Praise for S

"Max Yeh has brought to nary cultural convergenc reconstructing the miracu. tween the Prince of Wits and the Ten-Thousand. Emperor at the turn of the seventeenth century with a twenty-first-century twist. In the process, Yeh has plucked the sweet citrus of the Old and New Worlds, creating a translational space that uproots conventions and perceptions of East and West through the timelessness of storytelling, his pseudo-fictive madness akin to Sterne or Al-Mas'udi or Spence's *Emperor of China* or even the hallucinatory philosophical forays of Soviet outlier Krzhizhanovsky, though told in a nomadic style of his own soul-making, as he follows Christ among the Buddhists in Kashmir into the central kingdom before returning by way of a child's baseball mitt."

–JEFFREY YANG, author of *Vanishing-Line: Poems*

"Max Yeh's truly syncretic vision spans centuries and continents and various world literary traditions. I know of no other writer like him in Asian American literature."

–DOROTHY WANG, author of *Thinking Its Presence*

"Between the tragic Preface, with its terrifying first sentence, and the saddest reality of the Appendix lies the wonderful, great, reasoned epistolary struggle to make sense of life. Here, life itself is a fiction, and it is a fiction we all need to share..."

–DAVID COXHEAD, author of *Run Come See Jerusalem*

"This extraordinary 'pseudo-fiction' gives the reader history, mysteries, and discoveries as Max Yeh dares to write with exuberance in the voice of an Emperor of China and Miguel de Cervantes. Each describes his world of travels and philosophy of life in this exchange of letters, which Yeh threads together as a detective story hinting at discoveries of manuscript fragments..."

–DAVID RAY, author of *Hemingway: A Desperate Life*

STOLEN
ORANGES

20 19 18 17   4 3 2 1

Published by Kaya Press / www.kaya.com

Distributed by D.A.P./Distributed Art Publishers
(800)388-BOOK
www.artbook.com

ISBN: 978-1-885030-50-4
Library of Congress Control Number: 2017937419
Cover and book design: Nneka Bennett

This publication is made possible by support from the USC Dana and David
Dornsife College of Arts, Letters, and Sciences; and the USC Department
of American Studies and Ethnicity. Special thanks to the Choi Chang
Soo Foundation for their support of this work. Additional funding was
provided by the generous contributions of: Amna Akbar, Rahul and Erin
Banerjee, Luis Cabalquinto, Jade Chang, Lisa Chen & Andy Hsiao, Floyd
& Sheri Cheung, Prince Kahmolvat Gomolvilas, Jean Ho, Huy Hong,
Ramesh Kathanadhi, Helen Heran Kim, Juliana S. Koo, Pritsana Kootint-
Hadiatmodjo, Ed Lin, Viet Thanh Nguyen & Lan Duong, Chez Bryan Ong,
Whakyung Lee, Amarnath Ravva, Thaddeus Rutkowski, Duncan Williams,
Mikoto Yoshida, Amelia Wu & Sachin Adarkar, Anita Wu & James Spicer,
Patricia & Andy Yun, and others.

Kaya Press is also supported, in part, by: the National Endowment for the
Arts; the Los Angeles County Board of Supervisors through the Los Angeles
County Arts Commission; the City of Los Angeles Department of Cultural
Affairs; and the Community of Literary Magazines and Presses.

STOLEN ORANGES

LETTERS BETWEEN CERVANTES

and the EMPEROR OF CHINA

a pseudo-fiction

MAX YEH

Kaya Press

CONTENTS

"The style . . . presents the inconvenience we often have to complain of in Chinese books—vagueness in the ideas, often ambiguity in the expressions, and omission of the principal matters in the report, whilst some absurd details are minutely recorded. The indications of the geographical position of places are far from being precise, and the proper names are often corrupted. Besides this, many typographical blunders have crept [in] . . . which make it difficult for the reader to understand . . . ."

–E. BRETSCHNEIDER, *Medieval Researches From Eastern Asiatic Sources: Fragments Towards the Knowledge of the Geography and History of Central and Western Asia From the 13th to the 17th Century*

" . . . the habit of nearly all Chinese writers [is to incorporate] . . . bodily into their writings the work of others without giving the names either of the authors or of their books."

–F. HIRTH and W.W. ROCKHILL, eds., *Chu-fan-chi: Chinese and Arab Trade in the Twelfth and Thirteenth Centuries*

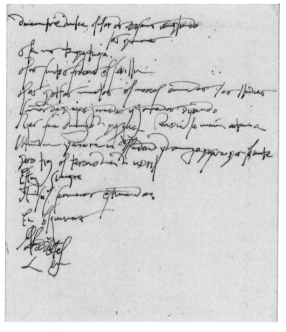

Figure 1. Last leaf of Cervantes's 1616 letter to the emperor, with his signature.

INTRODUCTION

I.

TEN YEARS AGO, A FEW DAYS AFTER CHRISTMAS, my wife, having fallen into a deep depression after a breakdown almost a year before, killed herself. The following spring, my demented mother died. She had had a series of mini-explosions in the subcortical region of her brain years before, leaving her with spotty memory and bizarre ratiocination. A week after her terrifying passing, my wife's mother also died. She, too, had been demented with an Alzheimer-like lapsus. It was then, when I was contemplating the insanity of life and, in the dark hours of insomnia, reading about the melancholia of Don Quixote, that I wondered who but a madman would believe that, at the beginning of the seventeenth century, the emperor of China and

Cervantes carried on a personal correspondence.

The Great Ming Emperor Wanli was more remote from his people and even from his own court than any other emperor in China's long history. Why would he write to Miguel de Cervantes, who, though famous to us now as the author of *Don Quixote*, was to the emperor an unknown writer in a tiny, unknown country at the far, unknown ends of the earth? This curious event seems even more extraordinary when we consider that, although China had had dealings with the European peoples for at least two thousand years, and although during the Middle Ages trade and travelers moved regularly between east and west, facilitated both by Persian and Arab intermediaries and by colonies of European merchants in Chinese trade cities, those direct relations had almost died out by the sixteenth century, shipwrecked Portuguese sailors being the only recorded Europeans in China until Portuguese traders landed in the Pearl River Delta at the beginning of the century. The immediate, historical circumstances for this epistolary exchange can be traced to the arrival of Jesuit missionaries in Macao towards the end of the century and, twenty years later, the appearance of two of them at the emperor's Forbidden City in 1601. This evangelical undertaking marked the beginning of European attempts to westernize China, which continue to this day, and so we might see the emperor's letters as a private and direct counter-incursion into European culture at the very moment Europe was beginning to impress itself upon the Chinese.

Such a view would seem to attribute god-like prescience to the emperor. And yet this Ming emperor of the Wanli years (1573-1620), Zhu Yijün, was the very emperor who gave the Jesuits permission to evangelize in China, accepting their presence in Beijing and even at his court. And however surprising and unbelievable this correspondence, we have indubitable proof that it happened, for Cervantes describes his reception of the emperor's first letter in the Dedication of the *Second Part of Don Quixote*, a sequel to his enormously popular work written ten years prior, a sequel forced on him by his usual impecunious situation and the possibility of garnering some profits from a market that had been opened by a spurious sequel, a fake *Second Part*, which had appeared the previous year:

> ... I get a huge number of urgent requests from all parts of the world to send them Don Quixote to ward off the revulsion and nausea caused by that fake Don Quixote who runs around the globe disguised as the Second Part, and the one who has shown the greatest desire has been the great Emperor of China, since, it is now a month ago, he wrote me in Chinese a letter brought by one of his own men, asking me, or I should say, begging me to send him Don Quixote, because he wanted to found a school for learning

Spanish and the book they were to read was to be
The History of Don Quixote. In addition to this,
he told me that I was to be the rector of this college.

I asked the messenger if his Majesty had given some-
thing to help in my expenses. He answered that he
hadn't given it even a thought.

"Then, brother," I replied, "you can go back to your
China by fast post or slow post or by whatever
post you came, because I am not healthy enough
to undertake such a long voyage, and further-
more, above and beyond being ill, I am very much
without money, and for all your emperors and all
your monarchs, I have in Naples the great Count
of Lemos, who without tittle-titles of colleges and
rectorships, sustains me, shelters me, and shows me
more kindnesses then I can desire."

We can date, then, the arrival of the emperor's messenger—a strange apparition this Chinese mandarin must
have been—to the end of September or possibly the
beginning of October in 1615, less than a year before
Cervantes's death. By then, Cervantes had finished the
Second Part, and Juan de la Cuesta, his printer, who had
already set type and pulled proofs for most of the book,
was urging him to finish the introductory pieces and
make arrangements for both government licenses and

church approvals. Cervantes might have been working that very day on his forgery of a censor's approval (though no evidence exists of such a forgery, except for the fact that Cervantes's book was finally prefaced with three such approvals instead of the required two), for which, over the signature of a non-existent Márquez Torres, he wrote a long and elaborate praise of himself, describing his fame abroad in France, Italy, Germany, and Flanders, and decrying, through the supposed voice of French gentlemen visitors to Spain, the national shame of his poverty.

The traditional interpretation of this Dedication to Count Lemos was stated by the great hispanist Americo Castro in his late work *Cervantes y los casticismos españoles* and popularized by Amelia Agostino de del Rio in her *Compañero del estudiante de Quijote.* Castro views the passage as a pointed irony directed at the Count, Pedro Fernando de Castro, probably no relation, who was the Count of Lemos as well as, among other things, the Viceroy, Governor, and Captain General of Naples and the President of the Supreme Court of Italy, and who had disappointed Cervantes in his expectations of being taken to Naples as a private secretary when the Count became the Viceroy, the Count having taken instead Bartolomé Leonardo de Argensola, known in the writing circles of Madrid as the "Rector of Villahermosa." Castro adds that the Count did indeed found a university in Naples, as Cervantes says the Chinese emperor intended. But even though Castro's interpretation is almost universally accepted by Cervantistas, I have viewed such coincidences with suspicion, since it leads to an absurdity in the context of a dedication; more than that, by praising so publicly the grace of a person who has not indeed been gracious, and by rejecting an offer that was not proffered, it implies a nasty sarcasm. I see no reason not to take Cervantes's word literally (and, indeed, how could one prove otherwise?), and so I have looked in the endless archives of imperial China for the letters that the emperor and Cervantes might have exchanged, and, having found almost the complete set of them, I herewith present them, thus making the argument over the Dedication a moot point.

II

ACCEPTING WHAT CERVANTES TELLS US AS TRUE—taking the visit of the Chinese messenger to be real—allows us to imagine that extraordinary scene and to wonder at the concatenation of histories that brought these two people together. For Cervantes, despite a life lived, he felt, constantly facing the variety, possibility, and disparity of human experience—having been years in foreign wars, having been years a captive among the Moors, having traveled all the roads of Spain with all the other travelers—destitute soldiers, pickpockets and murderers and prostitutes, merchants, donkey drivers, milkmaids, runaways, lovers, actors and singers, healers, madmen, barbers, clergy both local and returned from overseas, students, Muslims, Jews, forbidden sectarians—and having listened to all their stories—still, that morning in those first cool days of autumn in 1615 when he learned of the Wanli Emperor must have seemed to him bizarre beyond understanding.

He, of course, had no idea what a Chinaman was, much less what China was, though he might have heard of Tartars or Khitais, and although, in Algiers, he had seen a vast variety of peoples from the east and from Africa. Still, strangers would have looked strange to him, so to Cervantes, the foreign messenger's round face would have seemed, especially through his bulbous, fried-egg reading glasses, a mask with no topography, the eyes not receding into the skull but resting on the same plane as the nose, the nose not protruding any more than the full lips, so that the man peered out as if through two almond-shaped holes cut in tightly stretched pergamon, flat and wide and helmet-like, for his head was almost bald, and though the dark eyes darted here and there quickly, greeting Cervantes with intelligence, the man neither smiled nor showed any other emotion. He was not Turk nor Moor nor Arab, and though he wore the black cassock and short cape of a Jesuit, he did not look like any Christian Cervantes had ever seen.

Perhaps he had for the moment forgotten that he had seen men from the Extreme Orient before, almost thirty years before, when, not long after his marriage to Catalina—they were still living in Esquivias—he'd gone to Madrid because of his father's death, and, pushing through a crowd in front of the Puerto del Sol, he'd caught a glimpse of two beardless Japanese princes (he was later told there were four of them) being escorted by a host of Jesuits and courtiers. The four eminent converts from Francisco Xavier's mission in the east had spent years preparing and being groomed for their voyage to the west by the Society in Macao, where they had been taught European languages, sometimes by a young Italian named Matteo Ricci, who subsequently would take the word of God into China (one of the two Jesuits who arrived at the emperor's palace in Beijing in 1601) and who plays a major role in the story of this correspondence between the Wanli Emperor and Cervantes. Donald Lach's *Asia in the Making of Europe* describes the difficult, shipwrecked voyage of the four Japanese princes to Europe, and Jonathan Spence hints vaguely of the possible contact they had with Ricci in *The Memory Palace of Matteo Ricci*.

We get some idea of what Cervantes saw in the streets of Madrid in 1586 from a painting now hanging in the vestibule of the Teatro Olimpico in Vicenza, Italy that represents the visit of the four Japanese princes to the Teatro: they wear European clothes, and they sit in the first row by the proscenium stage, staring blankly at the suddenly vanishing illusions of the world's first perspectival stage set, a construction that was to be the source for theatre design and dramatic writing for hundreds of years, and that was also, in fact, a source for Cervantes's own much-discussed perspectivism in *Don Quixote*.

But we can now return to that ground-floor apartment in Madrid at the corner of the Calle Leon and the Calle de Francos, now called Calle de Cervantes, into which Cervantes and Catalina had moved the month before, the last of many, many displacements, since Cervantes was to die here six months later, ministered to by the clergyman son of the landlord who lived upstairs. The place was newly plastered, still smelling sweetly pungent from the lime, the windows of the main room, the only room besides the vestibule and the kitchen, looking out onto a small, seedy patio and an abandoned barn, and, across the patio, onto the *mentidero*, or fibber's corner, where actors would gather to practice their roles or audition for parts, for this apartment, like Cervantes's other recent homes, was in Madrid's squalid theatre district.

Standing just inside the doorway to the vestibule, the messenger explained, in an awkward and exaggerated Andalusian Spanish that was sibilated like Portuguese, that he had been sent by the Heavenly Son Figured in One Man to deliver a letter, and he proceeded to produce from the wide sleeves of his robe a small roll of paper, which he held out to Cervantes with both hands while bowing from the waist.

The paper was crumpled and soft, almost like a very thin and delicate felt, like nothing Cervantes had ever handled before, and he wondered that it was not blotched and torn by the quill as, laying the roll on top of his morning's work, he held one edge with his stump while unrolling it with his hand. The writing, if it was writing, since no quill could make such marks, was a series of swirling and blotched vertical columns of red lines that grew fat and turned upon themselves or tapered to thin drifts, all clustered in clumps, curiously reminding him of his father's old-fashioned script. In one corner, a series of darker red squares filled with hieroglyphical lines stood sentinel to the charted city. And while he listened to the priest, who was reading the letter out loud, intoning regular bursts of nasal, falsetto whines that dipped and rose with the nodding of his head, his surprise drifted into a certainty that someone was playing an elaborate joke on him; perhaps they had cooked up the scheme at the *mentidero*, though the question of where they could possibly have found this Japanese actor startled his certainty until he remembered that he had heard of Chinese and Japanese slaves being sold in Lisbon, the Asian slave trade having flourished throughout the second half of the sixteenth century alongside the growth of trade with China and Southeast Asia and the opening of the Jesuit missions, whose policy was to further trade by honoring property contracts and thus to return escaped slaves.

The Wanli Emperor, translated the messenger priest, who suddenly seemed very small to Cervantes, invites him to China to be a member of the Hanlin Academy in the Imperial City with a *jin shi* degree, there to teach in a special section for the Castilian tongue, or so we must surmise, since the full text of this first letter by Zhu Yijün has not been recovered. In the Appendix, I present translations from the Mongolian of the few extant fragments of this letter that were discovered, truly fortuitously, in Baku on the shores of the Caspian Sea in the nineteenth century, their presence in the southernmost part of the Russian empire being the indirect result of the explorations of the Jesuit Benedetto de Gois, who, in 1602, set off from Goa in India to walk to China through what is now Afghanistan. Three years later, Benedetto reached Xüzhou in western China, ill, abandoned by his bearers, and stripped of his clothing by robbers, and there, in 1607, Matteo Ricci found him and took him, dying, to Beijing, thus proving finally to the European world that the China to which Ricci had brought Christianity was indeed the same place that Marco Polo had called Cathay when talking to his bored cell-mates in a Genoan jail three hundred years before. Since the first of the Wanli Emperor's letters was written at about this same time—that is, shortly after *Don Quixote*'s arrival in China a few years after its publication in Spain in 1605—it seems likely that the emperor chose to send one copy of his letter along the old silk road as well as, following the Jesuits' usual practice, another copy, in Spanish, to Seville through Manila, Acapulco, Mexico, and Havana, and a third, in Portuguese, through Macao, Goa, Madagascar, and Lisbon. Clearly, the messenger priest whom Cervantes received in his small room with a sleeping alcove had come by one of the sea routes, though Cervantes seems to have been under the impression that he had arrived by post stations overland since, in the passage from his Dedication translated above that describes their meeting, he uses the expression "a las diez, o a las veinte, o a las que venis despachando," which I understand to refer to the distance between post stations.

Whatever the two talked about, the priest had to have convinced Cervantes that he was no fake messenger, that he came from a nameless country, called simply "the empire" by its natives and identified only as belonging to the Ming, who ruled over a land one and a half times the size of Europe and fifteen times the size of Spain, and that this country lay far, far to the east, according to the *mapamundi* that Father Barndoor Li had made and set up on six six-foot panels in the emperor's chambers. In referring to Ricci, the messenger priest would have used the Chinese name that Ricci had created for himself by adapting the sounds of his Italian name to a Chinese motto espousing his personal undertaking in life—that of opening up the barn of China to the horses of instruction—a method of translated self-naming much like the emblematic *imprese* that were all the rage in Italy in the sixteenth century, which Ricci reinvented in a new context and which the missionaries in China all subsequently emulated, the Chinese messenger priest feeling both a hang-head reverence and a guilty glee at the comicality of the name thus used, not knowing that Ricci had already been dead five years as he spoke it.

He said that the distance was so great and the way passing through so many other and diverse countries that it had taken him eight years to bring Cervantes the emperor's letter; that this was not even so bad, since he knew of a letter that took seventeen years to reach Europe from China; that the emperor of China was the son of heaven, which was not to be confused with Yesu the Resurrected; that, in spite of the fact that the emperor had not mentioned money, there was no problem with household expenses for this emperor, who had spent eight million Mexican silver dollars to build his tomb when he was a young man of twenty-two; that the offer was not only serious but, given the nature of the emperor of China, absolute; that he himself was from the southern part of the empire and had been converted and baptized early in the mission's work in China by the Portuguese father Eyes Fixed on Jesus; that he had learned Spanish from Father I Follow Confused, who had been born near Seville—the same year, it seems, that Cervantes had, on his name day, lost his hand at the battle of Lepanto—and who had attended the same Jesuit College in Seville founded by Ignatius Loyola where Cervantes—surprised at this—had also studied; that the emperor's curiosity in Cervantes had been piqued not only by reading *Don Quixote*, but also by Father Barndoor Li's suggestion that he himself might possibly have had an indirect acquaintance with its author—which surprised Cervantes even more—in that in 1572, when he was studying in Rome and Lepanto was still talked about everywhere, since people were wondering if that spring would, as in previous years, once more see the Turks renew their threat to Christian nations, he had, in walking past the Ospedali di S. Tomaso not far from Claudius's aqueduct, met an old friend from his home town of Macerata whom he had not seen for several years. The priest then went on to tell Cervantes the following account of Ricci's story:

III.

ON AN ASSIGNMENT FROM THE GREAT REFORMER and later sanctified Filippo Neri to consider the ruins of the Santa Maria in Vallicella as a possible site for a new oratorio for his growing congregation, Barndoor Li, then only a young novitiate of nineteen, was striding muscularly past the hospital when he saw a friar hesitantly descend the hospital steps leaning on a crutch. The man's unfamiliarity with his long stick, his weakened legs, and the pallor of his face showed that he had recently been released from the hospital and was convalescing from a serious illness or injury, so that Barndoor looked at the man with some compassion and dwelled on his features a little more than he normally would have.

"Ruggero, Ruggero," he called out suddenly, crossing himself when he finally recognized his friend. "What are you doing in Rome? What has happened to you? Look at you, so skinny and wan, you look like a ghost. Come, come let me help you."

Fra Ruggero, whom Spence mentions in his study of Ricci, blinked in the sunlight at seeing Barndoor.

"Matteo," he said.

The two friends hugged, and as Barndoor helped Fra Ruggero down the steps, the friar explained briefly how he, with others from Macerata, had served at the battle of Lepanto, where he had been wounded while ministering to the injured and dying on-board a Neapolitan ramming galley named the *Marquesa*—startling Cervantes again. And since Fra Ruggero had often had to describe the battle, he elaborated easily and in detail the horrors of the battle, the movements of the ships, the lines held and broken, the strategies, feints, and driving attacks, the successes and failures of commanders and of men, the great noise of the cannons and harquebuses, the way the boardings took place, the placement of the men, their desperation when they engaged, knowing full well that once locked to the other ship, they would all die unless they vanquished, so that, roaring with pain and fear, they fought to their last breath and often beyond, the blood, the entrails on which you could fatally lose your footing, the hands blown off, the eyeless faces and blood and screams everywhere, and then the smoky silence in which one could not tell if we had won or lost the day.

The two men decided not to stand in the street talking all day and so went together to hear mass at San Llorente—the China person here mixing up his languages, Cervantes noticed—and afterwards to Barndoor's, where they shared a few rolls and some sausages made from Rute ham as Barndoor had promised, and, after finishing the meal, Barndoor asked his friend to continue telling him what he had been doing.

Fra Ruggero began by saying that while it was true he was suffering from wounds he had received at Lepanto, he had not been a patient at San Tomás, but rather had been recently released—coincidentally, since he had just heard of Barndoor's connection with Filippo Neri—from Neri's Convalescenziario, that he had been at San Tomás to visit a young Spanish soldier named Miguel de Cervantes, whom he had cared for during the battle and later in the General Hospital at Messina, this Miguel having been a harquebusman at the bow of the ship Ruggero had served on and having lost his left hand and been delirious from that and other wounds to his chest.

At this point in the priest's story, Cervantes exclaimed, "But that is true! I remember a young Italian friar who came to see me at the hospital several times, but I've forgotten his name, if I ever knew it. My God, this is extraordinary!" And he begged the priest to continue, which the priest did, saying that Fra Ruggero told Barndoor he was much concerned about Cervantes because that very day Cervantes had told him a story that could not be believed. He did not know what to make of it, because Cervantes had sworn it to be true, but perhaps Miguel was mad, and when pressed to tell the story, Ruggero protested that he had already told Barndoor of extraordinary, excessive events that defied the imagination, and if he were to tell him what Miguel claimed to have seen, Barndoor would think that all his stories were mere fabrications. But Barndoor, who was naturally persuasive, humoured him, praised him, and gently prodded him into telling Miguel's story.

It seems that, as Barndoor himself had seen, when the brothers of the Capuchino order go out in the evening to beg, they take with them two dogs who carry lanterns in their mouths to light the way, and, as coins are thrown out the windows, the dogs trot over to where the coins land, lighting them up to show the brothers. These two dogs, named Scipio and Berganza, though gentle as lambs in the street, mount guard at the Hospital as if fierce lions. Well, the night before last, Miguel had said—and Cervantes already knew what the messenger priest would say—stretched out sweating on an old, stained mat, dark and shadowy in moonlight, lying awake thinking of his past happiness and present suffering, he heard some voices talking in the middle of the night, and, peering into the dark, he'd slowly realized that the speakers were those two dogs, Scipio and Berganza.

"I wrote that story," interrupted Cervantes, "and I heard them not just that night but for many nights after, and the dogs themselves were as surprised as I was that they could suddenly talk. They argued about how they could remember events and even thoughts from before the time they could speak. I recorded it all."

And indeed he was right. The "Coloquio que pasó entre Cipion y Berganza," part of the story "El Casamiento Engañoso" that is collected in Cervantes' *Novelas Ejemplares,* recounts the autobiographies of these two dogs as told to one another in the dead of night.

Barndoor thought that Miguel must have been dreaming, but Fra Ruggero said that Miguel had heard the dogs again the following night, when he'd been careful to be awake. The two then argued long into the night about Miguel's sanity and the possibility or impossibility of dogs talking, one maintaining that God's order of creation forbade it, the other insisting that God's will and power overruled that hierarchy, and surely animals spoke in the Garden, since they all seemed to have understood the names that Adam had given them, though God had taken speech away from them after the Transgression, but why would God take the ability to speak away from all the animals if only the snake was guilty, and did God take away only the vocal ability of animals or all of their intellect and comprehension of language with it, and did not the birds speak to one another in their language, and what about dogs, who obey their masters' commands, and what about parrots, though theirs is an aped speech and not real. The heat and length of that argument, and the curiosity of its subject, set the incident firmly in Barndoor's memory, so that, years later, in another world and another time, when he presented the emperor with a copy of *Don Quixote,* he accompanied the book with an account of his meeting with Fra Ruggero.

IV.

Cervantes listened in wonderment at the coincidences that had taken this story about himself to the ends of the earth and back again, but neither he nor the priest knew that Ricci might have known Cervantes even more directly than his story to the emperor indicated. Indeed, Ricci himself did not know that he knew.

In 1568, Giulio Acquaviva, then only twenty-one years old, but, because of his family, already chamberlain to Pope Pius V, was sent to Felipe II in Madrid on a papal mission. The following year, he is said to have brought Cervantes back to Rome with him—apparently at the behest of his friend Gaspar de Cervantes y Gaete (no relation, despite the shared name), the Cardinal of Tarragon—in order to protect Cervantes from charges of attempted murder, the punishment for which was the loss of a hand. However, many scholars now dispute this story, since, in 1569, only three months after the issuance of a warrant for the arrest of Miguel de Cervantes that has since been discovered in the Simancas Archives, Alonso Getino Guzman, chief constable of Madrid, issued a certificate attesting to the purity of Cervantes's Christian blood, a document Cervantes needed in order to join the army. So it seems there must have been two Miguel de Cervantes at the time in Madrid. Those doubting scholars who think that Cervantes went to Italy on his own at this time must deal with the lengthy arguments of the learned Luis Astrana Marín in his six-volume *Vida Ejemplar y Heroica de Miguel de Cervantes y Saavedra.*

Still, perhaps because of this introduction to Giulio Acquaviva by Cardinal Gaspar de Cervantes y Gaete (not to be confused with his grand-nephew, Gaspar de Gaete y Cervantes, whom Cervantes came to know intimately forty years later), Cervantes served Giulio, who was a year older than he, as chamberlain—or as page, say some—after Giulio became a cardinal in 1570. Or so Cervantes himself claims in his Prologue to *La Galatea.*

Ricci, who had come to Rome in 1568 to study law, might well have been a frequent visitor to Giulio's house in those years just prior to his joining the Society of Jesus, since he was intimate with Giulio's uncle Claudio, who was only three years older than Giulio, and especially with Giulio's brother Rodolfo, who was about Ricci's age. In the period we are concerned with, this illustrious Neapolitan family (which still gathers from time to time for a scholarly conference dedicated to the study of its history; see, for example, *Atti del sesto Convegno: gli Acquaviva d'Aragon: duchi di Atri e conti di S. Flaviano*) counted amongst its members five cardinals, two archbishops, a general of the Society of Jesus, and a saint. Claudio Acquaviva joined the Society of Jesus in 1567. In 1581, he became its general—some say the greatest of all its generals—and one of his first duties was to send Ricci to Macao with the idea of penetrating into China. His nephew, Giulio's brother Rodolfo, joined the order in 1568, the year he first met Ricci, and Ricci joined in 1571, a few months before the battle of Lepanto. So not only were Ricci and the Acquavivas novitiates together in Rome, but Rodolfo and Ricci both served together in Goa, where, in the city of Salcete, having successfully finished a mission to the Great Moghul Akbar, Rodolfo was martyred shortly after Ricci left for Macao and China.

Still, though Cervantes might have seen and even talked with Ricci at Giulio's house on those occasions when these wealthy and powerful young men would gather casually, he had no way of knowing that the Barndoor Li of the priest's account was Matteo Ricci. And, for his part, Ricci never knew the name of the Cardinal's young attendant, and so did not know, when talking with his friend Fra Ruggero about the colloquy of dogs, that he already knew its narrator. Thus when the Chinese priest took leave of Cervantes that day, neither knew of this other web that had been woven between the lives of the two men. And, finally, it did not matter—nor did it matter to either man that, at the time of their interview, Claudio Acquaviva lay dying in Rome.

V.

I HAVE NO IDEA WHO THE MESSENGER PRIEST WAS who
spoke with Cervantes for such a long time that day in
1615, though his mention of Su Ruwang or João Soerio
as his spiritual father suggests that he might have been
Joseph, Melchior, Gaspard, or Balthazar, the baptized
members of the little group, run by Soerio, that was
secretly meeting in Nanjing. Yet, since he learned
Spanish from Pang Diwo (Diego de Pantoja) and was
the emperor's man, he seems to have been from Beijing
in the north. The records of the Society do not show
any member of the Nanjing congregation—all sons of
the local prince—as having been ordained, however,
and indeed, there are no records of any converts having
been accepted into the ministry in those early years of
the mission. So the letter-bearer may have entered the
order somewhere along his eight-year voyage, like the
traveling companion of the discrete and self-effacing
Chinese Christian monk Sima Laban, or like Marcos,
who traveled in the thirteenth century from China to
Tabriz and Teheran, perhaps crossing paths with the
Marco from Italy, and who, in Persia, became a priest,
and very soon after, the Patriarch of the Nestorian
Christian Church. Or the messenger might not have
been a true priest at all, donning the robes only as a
kind of disguise to make his travel in Europe somewhat
easier and safer, for in Europe, unlike in the countries

to the east, foreigners, especially dark-complexioned strangers, were killed, imprisoned, cast into insane asylums, expelled, or enslaved, as those Chinese who escaped from Gibraltar, where the Spanish had transported tens of thousands of Chinese troublemakers captured in the Philippines, discovered.

I have also been unable to discover what became of this messenger priest subsequent to his interview with Cervantes in Madrid, whether he was the anonymous author of the work called *Sketch of the Countries, People, and Products West of the Border*, which traces an itinerary between Jiayü on the northwest border of China and Lumi or Rome, as Constantinople was sometimes called, or whether, like Sima Laban, he visited the royal courts of France and England, celebrated Easter mass with the Pope in Rome, sold papal indulgences in Veroli, returned to China to die quietly, and was buried behind the imperial palace, where an emperor might burn incense for him two hundred years later as the Wanli Emperor still did at Sima Laban's grave. Or indeed whether, like Arcade Huang, another Chinese voyager to Europe, he married a French girl, the daughter of his landlord, I believe, lived an impoverished, sad, lonely, quiet life in a walk-up flat on the Rue du Seine in Paris, and attempted to make a grammar and a much-maligned linguistic system for classical Chinese, a language he himself did not know well. Or if, instead, like the effervescent Hu, who was called Don Quixote in Port Louis, and whose nostalgia and misunderstandings closed him in so tightly that his struggles to find a little peace and justice were mistaken for madness, with the result that he was committed to the asylum at Charenton, and, perhaps, made to play the role of the Chinese emperor in a Marquis de Sade production, sitting dazed in his corner, draped in the one blanket he'd been given, then leaping up suddenly to slash at the air with his toy sword.

VI.

AS FOR CERVANTES, WE MAY SEEM TO KNOW much about him from the hundreds of biographies and thousands of studies that have been written about him, but the indubitable documents that tell us something of his activities are really quite few: a recorded baptism on the 7th of October 1547; a document, locating him in Rome at the age of 22, which guarantees that he and his family have always been Christians and were not converted Jews, and thus that his blood is pure enough for him to be accepted into the army; legal documents that connect him, circuitously, to Cardinal Giulio Acquaviva; legal declarations that describe his participation in the battle of Lepanto, which are attached to a request for a pension or other recompense not yet received; twelve depositions taken in Algeria by Fray Juan Gil, the Trinitarian procurator who ransomed Cervantes from Algerian pirates in 1580 after five years of captivity, depositions that respond to accusations made by the Dominican Juan Blanco de Paz of Cervantes's cowardly and perfidious and perhaps immoral actions while a prisoner by asserting Cervantes's heroism and altruism and leadership, but that also suggest incredible luck and favoritism; a letter to the Council of Indies requesting a position in America in 1590, which was rejected, he is now 42 years old; an order by Francisco Moscoso, which places him in jail in Castro del Rio in

1592 for demanding more grain than he was entitled to as royal grain requisitioner for the Spanish Armada's expedition against England; a contract with Rodrigo Osorio in Seville for a series of plays; ordination papers that he witnessed for his brother-in-law Juan in Toledo; first prize in a poetry contest in Zaragosa in 1595; incarceration papers, issued in Seville in 1597, detailing charges by the crown that, as dunning official for the crown, tasked with collecting tax arrears, he has not met his quota; a registry of residence in Valladolid; incarceration papers from Valladolid in 1605, the year *Don Quixote* is published, for the murder of Gaspar de Ezpeleta, a charge from which he is eventually exonerated, and he is now 57; various changes of address registered in Madrid's Corte de los Austrias district beginning in 1606; and documents regarding his burial in 1616 in the Trinitarian monastery where he was a novitiate.

While such documentation may speak to us loudly of an extraordinarily eventful life, it also leaves much unsaid, and even whispers *sotto voce* of an unusually ambiguous and even duplicitous style of existence. Cervantes's life, and indeed the lives of all the members of his family, is a house of cards built of legal contentions, accusations, declarations and affidavits, sworn testimonies (much of them false), counter-claims, clever legal strategies, contracts, and litigations. His mother swears that she is a widow in order to petition for his ransom money, but is joined by his father in her next petition. Cervantes files lengthy sworn testimonies to support his request for a government pension, but uses his brother Rodrigo's service documents. His aunt and his sisters and his daughter, sometimes joined by Cervantes, repeatedly bring suits against various lovers for breach of promise and for paternity; in fact, this method seems to be their main source of income. Cervantes's father's personal property is saved from confiscation for payment of a debt by his sister Andrea's notarized affidavit that the property is hers, a ploy that is used by Cervantes to protect his daughter Isabela's house from creditors, though, in a secret contract, he deeds the house back to his friend and Isabela's former lover, the person from whom Isabela had originally gotten the house in the first place as part of a settlement. Isabela sues Cervantes for it, and the issue drags on for years after his death. In 1589, Cervantes appears in Seville with a large sum of money that he uses to buy cloth, something the family seems to have done often as a method for banking cash, but when he is charged with embezzlement, he manages to elude the charge. Even when taking vows with the Third Order of the Franciscans, the Trinitarians, his sister Andrea falsely swears that she is the widow of some non-existent gentleman, a General Alvaro Mendaño. So we do not really know how Cervantes behaved in battle or as a prisoner, whether he was an authentic Christian or a converted Jew, whether he embezzled funds from the state or was the scapegoat of disgruntled farmers, whether he cheated the crown out of taxes or was a victim of bad arithmetic. Yet among scholars today, his life, lived on the streets with wit, stratagem, and opportunism, still seems exemplary and heroic and even truthful, for like all hustlers and conmen, he charms us with his cheer and resilience.

Even if it should be proven that Cervantes never went to Italy, that he never fought in the battle of Lepanto but was instead that other Miguel de Cervantes, the one mentioned in the Simancas document who stabbed the mason Antonio de Sigura in a knife scuffle, who was caught, tried, and had his hand mutilated before being sent to the galleys, which he survived only to be taken by corsairs to Algeria, where he was miraculously reunited with his brother Rodrigo, who, on his way home from service in Naples, had also been captured by Algerian pirates; even if his life were that of the mysterious Gines de Pasamontes—galley slave, novelist, puppet-play producer, robber of Sancho Panza's ass—who so strangely keeps reappearing in both Parts of *Don Quixote*, though in different disguises and under different names; even so, Cervantes could hardly be considered mean-spirited, dishonest, a scoundrel or a thief, only that he gave himself readily to circumstances as they presented themselves, that he was quick to find an advantage, that he always had a ready response to questions and situations, that he was self-aware and had that verbal gift of explanation, rationalization, repartee, and method that God has given to city dwellers. Circumstances may have forced him into regrets for actions taken or not taken—that, though he brought his illegitimate, newborn daughter Isabela into his home immediately after he married Catalina, neither he nor Catalina really cared for her (he suggests to the emperor that she was not his daughter), that he never taught her to read, that he indentured her to his sister Magdalena, that he pawned her off on first one man and then another in order to try to arrange her marital interests—yet he remained stubbornly loyal and honest, despite not having the time, leisure, or interest to consider morality separate from the exigencies of life or his ironic stance towards it.

In Cervantes's time, such a picaresque struggle for survival was common. The medieval economy, with its hierarchic basis on land ownership, still persisted, and the new money economy, only a hundred years old in Spain at that time, was not strong enough to support the masses of people who were no longer bound to the land, with the result that all those who were neither landowners with livelihoods secured upon inherited land, nor peasants whose livelihoods were equally and slavishly fixed to their labour on that land—that is, all those who were neither Don Quixote nor Sancho Panza—found no pecuniary support. Their education and social contacts, their aspirations and abilities, their habits and tastes were socially and culturally in the middle, between the peasant and the aristocrat, yet there was no economic basis for a middle class, capitalism not yet having created an industrial and mercantile economy that could support the people in the middle, and so they were outsiders to the existing economic structure and lived off the refuse heap of that economy. They served both ends of the scale, were clerks and secretaries, debt collectors and notaries, playwrights, innkeepers, servants, stewards, village priests, barbers and surgeons, soldiers, students, prostitutes and entertainers, seamstresses, constables, and witches: toadies and conmen, all. Their lives—amorphous, complex, viciously competitive, passionate, schizophrenic, contentious, legally and amorously embroiled—ground the feudal world into dust and created the modern world. Both Shakespeare and Cervantes came from this group, and it was out of this milieu, too, that Columbus emerged. And in fact one of Cervantes's relatives on his grandmother Leonora Fernandez de Torreblanca's side even shipped with Columbus, dying among those abandoned at La Navidad. For three generations, the men in Cervantes's family had been forced to leave or had simply abandoned their wives and children to wander, largely within the country, looking for opportunities and jobs. Cervantes himself was away in the south for fourteen years working at various occupations that never paid him enough to live on, much less to support his family.

Yet the family stayed bonded, and even took in all those at its peripheries. At various times, Cervantes's household included his abandoned and demented grandmother Leonora, his father's abandoned sister Maria de Mendoza, his abandoned mother, another Leonora—de Cortinas—who also became demented, and, later, his abandoned sister Andrea and her illegitimate daughter Constanza, his other abandoned sister, Magdalena, his own illegitimate daughter, Isabela, Juana Gaitan, the widow of his friend the poet Láinez, and his own wife, Catalina. Indeed, when Cervantes moved to the apartment on the corner of the Calle de Leon and the Calle de Francos, where he met the emissary from China, he and Catalina were living alone for the first time in their lives, Constanza having moved out only a year before and his sisters dead or in the nunnery.

While the variety, exuberance, and energy of these lives, caused by a mismatch between the social order and the economic structure, may lead us to think of them as expansive, free, and available, yet that openness was experienced as a terrible constraint, and Cervantes saw its circle tighten around the lives of all the women of his family. There was nothing to do in life, no way to make a living, no function to fulfill, no desires to satisfy, no self to construct, no way to go day by day towards death except to find a man, and so, for women in this yet-to-be middle class, the focus of life was to attract a suitable husband, to attract by the turn of an ankle beneath a coyly lifted skirt, to attract by the flash of mascara-accented eyes, to attract by hauntingly low laughter, the brush of a perfumed glove or hand-kerchief, the suggestive arch of a back, always holding out as ultimate attraction the proffered apple. Unlike the medieval tradition of courtly love, which purified its passions by distinguishing itself from marriage, thus disdaining property and legality, this early modern form of sexual relations was aimed at marriage and was thus sunk in practicality and calculation: methodical, legal, and material.

Central to this feminine world of courtship, love, and sex—powerful controller of women's destinies and source of life and livelihood—was the matchmaker, the Celestina figure of Fernando de Rojas's play *La Comedia de Calisto y Melibea*. Cervantes's sister Andrea fashioned herself such a position, and so was able to have her own home where, as "seamstress," she trained young women in the ways of the world—perhaps, like Celestina, teaching them how to seam broken hymens. She dealt in cloths, gave legal advice to her charges, placed young girls in service, fenced stolen goods from their masters' houses, midwifed their bastard children, dispensed herbs and wisdom, concocted henna hair dye, kohl and digitalis eye shadowing, and antimonic body powder, decocted essential oils of rose petals, lavender blooms, lime peels, and salvia leaves, practiced emergency surgery like her father, and, like her brother, had a ready response and a persuasive tongue. Doctor, lawyer, merchant, chief, botanist, alchemist, beggar, thief, she was all the professions. Knowing and inventive, she taught the *techne* of sexual attraction and created female beauty in clothes and cosmetics and perfumes. Such power did not go unthreatened. The arts and sciences of enchantment that women like Andrea kept alive for the modern world belonged to the dark mind that the Renaissance was trying to expurgate from the Middle Ages, and so, while these aromatic love potions brought welcome income, they also stimulated accusations of witchcraft that the frequent spectacles of faith produced by the Inquisition (and attended by Andrea) showed were often heeded. More serious still were the spiritual threats, for in the liquid world of circumstantial priorities, the matchmaker shades into the procuress as the would-be bride easily becomes the kept woman and then the prostitute, a situation as real for Andrea as her life, the only remedy for which was to take vows, which she did, and, following her, Cervantes.

We see the influence of this woman's reality on Cervantes in his delight with the convoluted ways in which women pursue the resolution of their relations with men to find financial and emotional security. This pleasure and intent inform all the stories of delayed bliss that he interpolates throughout *Don Quixote* and that also make up the bulk of the *Novelas Ejemplares* as well as the plots of the hundreds of plays he wrote and the large, central issue at the heart of *Los Trabajos de Persiles y Sigismunda*. A young girl is kidnapped from her parents by a band of young nobles, is viciously raped and kept a prisoner in the ringleader's house, but manages to escape; over many years, she and her bastard son are able to bring the villain to true repentance and love, and she is finally made an honest woman in marriage. A beautiful gypsy girl disdains all the money and love poems that are thrown at her feet to purchase her favor; instead, she enjoins an adolescent nobleman among her crowd of suitors to leave home and become part of the gypsy band, where he adapts to the vagabond ethos and manages to become a leader and respected thief while maintaining his virtue by himself providing the money that he claims to have stolen; his equanimity is tested, as is the depth of his friendship; he matures and becomes worthy of love until, humiliated by false accusations and provoked by the lechery and deceit of his accuser, his nobility surfaces, and he kills in a fit of heroic rage; the gypsy girl, discovering that she is actually of noble birth and had been kidnapped by the gypsies, finds her true parents and, through them, saves the young man's life so that finally, with all the requisites in place, the two can be joined. The beautiful, intelligent, and virtuous daughter of well-to-do peasants is seduced by the importunate promises of the lascivious younger brother of her father's feudal lord, then is immediately abandoned by him; disguised as a boy, she follows him to a nearby town, where he is about to be married, but finds that he has stabbed his betrothed because she is in love with another and refuses to marry him; he escapes; she, trying to avoid being discovered by her parents, goes into the wilds with her servant, who, in the deep woods, tries to rape her; she succeeds in fending him off and wanders about the countryside, sometimes serving the locals as a shepherd boy, until chance brings her into such complex dealings with her seducer, his betrothed, and his betrothed's lover, that she is able to reform her repentant lover and marry him. Over and over, rape, seduction, and sex are triumphed over by ingenuity, persistence, and a little luck.

Though Cervantes depicts a reality of shifting fortunes in these extravagantly plotted stories, he thought of them as fantasies, which they are, fantasies set into motion by his belief in the twisting ironies of calamity and the labyrinthine ingenuities of those who could follow such devious pathways to a personal advantage. Thus his writings are characterized by complex and multiple plots that thread through each other, by many-layered narrative structures that open a spacious hall of deceptive mirrors and ironies, and by his exuberant, stylistic range, which displays that metropolitan quickness and sensitivity for language that he felt could create life and fortune. His eyes filled with glee when, disputing Sancho Panza's perception that Mambrino's golden helmet is really a barber's basin, Don Quixote says that it might be that someone in the past had not recognized the helmet as such and, seeing that it was made of gold, had cut it in half to sell the precious metal while making a barber's basin out of the remainder, for he has to admit that even to his eyes it looks like a basin, though he knows better and intends to have it remade into the shape of a helmet.

Yet, as the reader shall see, there is none of this spirit in the two letters that Cervantes writes to the emperor, none of this direct engagement with life, none of the gleeful one-upmanship, the bewildering deception, no vacillating, uncertain carnival. Rather we see Cervantes in deeply meditative self-reflection, speaking as if to himself, without the ironic, defensive pose of dialogue with which he usually engaged the world, for these letters are more soliloquy than correspondence, the distance in space, time, and culture being so great as to make any hoped-for response futile, thus isolating the letters from any context or history, as if the writing were free of events, even, perhaps, free of identity, something that Matteo Ricci understood when he wrote "I know not whether this my letter will find you in heaven or earth: but whatever the case, I want to write you" to his father, who, unbeknown to him, was already dead. Yet they are not entirely soliloquies, because they are directed at whomever he thought the emperor to be, someone whose own situation and being called him outside of himself.

VII.

THE CHINESE EMPEROR WAS CALLED *YIREN*, which might mean that he was the first in rank among men, or it might mean that he was unique and solitary, that while the rest of us are fathers or mothers, sons or daughters, brothers or sisters, friends, friends of friends, parts of a larger whole, of society, of a locality, of a clan, family, or association, of humanity, and thus not *yiren*, not unique and single, he was meant to stand in no human relation with anyone else. He, though mortal, was heaven's son, the one representative on earth of natural order, responsible by virtue of his uniqueness for mediating between heaven's (nature's) order and the chaos of our human existence, functioning by his every breath, his every movement, his every thought as regulator of peace and balance in the universe. So one can hardly think of him as exercising power in the Roman or Germanic notion of personal leadership of a people within geographic borders, which is not to say that he did not govern the people of China, only that he ruled within the structure and balance of belief, and only so long as he fulfilled his unique position within that structure and balance, and not because of his personal capacities. Like money, his inherent value was null, currency alone keeping him alive.

Everything about the Emperor Wanli distinguished him from others. His names—his family name Zhu or

Red; his personal given name, Yijün, the Great Potter; the name of his reign, Wanli, meaning Myriad Turnings of the Heavens, which he was also sometimes called; his temple name, Shen Zong, Divine Ancestors; the name derived from his tomb, Ding Ling; the name he gave himself for his literary and artistic productions, Yü Zhai, In the Beginning the Sun Rises Balanced Between the Earth and the Heavens; even the word *chen*, meaning "me," with which he referred to himself—all were expurgated from the language so no other person could use them. The five-colored porcelain, representing the five parts of the empire, the dishes and bowls and cups he used every day, were made for him alone at Kaolin mountain from a vitreous form of the white, edible clay prescribed for stomach disorders. The brushes of his scribe were of a unique flame-colored lacquer, *tung-wei*, and could be used only to write his words. The cloth of his clothes, the colors of his bedding, the contours of his toilet bowl, the strings of his *pipa*: none could be duplicated. This singularity allowed no variation and was like the unique patterns of the yarrow sticks in the casting of the *Yijing*, which, once thrown, enter into the totality of a complex, undecipherable, but assuredly linked entwinement of events so that, like butterfly wings whose movement generates, through innumerable connections of fluid and thermal flows, a storm of hail on the other side of the globe, the patterns of yarrow sticks can be read to indicate the state of all other events to which they are connected.

The emperor's life was the casting of the sticks; everything he did was assiduously studied and interpreted to discover the state of universal harmony. As he awoke each morning out of some unknown place of darkness—even before he opened his eyes or felt his body come into an existence of touch and warmth and an aching in the back of his knees and the crook of his arms—he was, we imagine, conscious that he had to lie quietly until the Ministry of Rites and the Directorate of Ceremonials determined which side of his bed he was to get up on, for every minute detail of his life was ritualized, coordinated, and orchestrated, conformed to antiquity or was prohibited if without precedent, aligned with the direction and strength of the winds that blew through his life, harmonized with the phases of the moon, the position of the sun, and the motions of the constellations that he revolved in concert with. When his mother, Lishi, the August Empress Dowager Cusheng, wanted to ask him to go to the theatre, she had to write him a message that would be transmitted through the palace delivery system and read to him by a member of the Hanlin Academy, the faculty of which Cervantes had been invited to join, while the emperor lay ceremoniously on the ground in submission, the letter then being filed with the state papers, entering thus into dynastic historian Chen Yübi's ongoing compilation of Ming history as it evolved moment by moment, the *Ming Shi*. And when the emperor finally took his mother and the August Empress Dowager Renshen to the theatre, he awaited their arrival on his knees in the courtyard in a ceremony of filial waiting that was produced for the occasion by the board of ceremonies and in which the roles of the immortals were played by hired actors, most of whom the emperor would have recognized but probably did not know by name. All these actions were recorded by Chen Yübi's agent, the scribe with the *tung-wei* brush who wrote out the emperor's invitation to Cervantes and who followed Wanli around day and night throughout his life, but whose name the Sun Balanced Between Earth and Heavens also did not know.

When Changlo, Wanli's first son, was born to one of his mother's maidservants, the Red Potter, then eighteen, stubbornly denied his paternity until he was read the relevant passages from the daybooks of the previous year, which are still extant, which narrate his discussions with Big Buddy Feng of his erections under the green-edged black dragon robe when he watched the girl prostrate before him, something about the slight sidewise movement of her hips distinguishing her from the others; that recorded Big Buddy's lessons on sexual practice, the eunuch massaging his penis until the uncontrollable spasms of ejaculations squeezed the tacky, white sperm from him; which describe in detail the image of the naked girl stripped behind a screen in his bedroom and carried, under the direction of Big Buddy, by two eunuchs to his bed where, standing on either side, they stroked the girl with camel-bird feathers, caressed her nipples with the tips of their long, gold-sheathed fingernails, and twitched her thighs lightly with thin bamboo rods until her vagina opened wide and soft and wet; and which tells how Big Buddy held his erect penis, directing it into her vagina as the two eunuchs lowered her onto him, of the sudden warmth around his penis and his inability to focus on anything but the straining of his penis, of his burst of sperm into the girl, who was being rocked on his stomach. He had to acknowledge that Changlo was his son, though he disliked saying so, disliked the boy, who became the next emperor in spite of his efforts against him, disliked the boy's mother, whom he designated First Imperial Consort and then confined to her quarters until she died thirty-three years later (though, unknown to him, her remains would be transferred to his tomb after his death), and disliked Big Buddy, even though the eunuch had been his only friend, ally, and confidant as a child, disliked him even more for that, and also because, after his execution, his house revealed valuables worth three times the imperial treasury. How the world's harmony had become unbalanced.

He entered this world at the age of eight, in 1563, in the first of the enthroning ceremonies, during which he appeared three times out of a screened cubicle set up in the enormous courtyard in front of the sun-facing gate, each time wearing a different hat and a different set of clothes, the patterns of which would constitute his dress for the rest of his life: first the rectangular mortar board with short edges front and back from which hung twelve beads, worn with a black jacket and yellow skirt and jade belt decorated with two tassels, as well as a rectangular knit apron matched with red socks and red ankle boots; then next a shell-like helmet of leather, feathers, and jewels with a chin strap, which was worn with a jacket and skirt in flaming red; and finally the yellow dragon robe, worn with a black, soft cap embroidered with dragons playing with a large pearl of a moon. Each time he stepped out of the cubicle, he said, "So be it," which was repeated by two heralds, then four, then eight, then sixteen, until the whole assembled court of ten thousand repeated his order.

In imagining the young emperor thus, we must not sentimentalize him in the popular western image of the child emperor that we see, for example, in Eisenstein's film *Ivan the Terrible* or in Bertolucci's re-use of that image in *The Last Emperor*, where a naive, confused, frightened, free spirit of a child is entrapped and distorted by an incomprehensible world of empty ceremony. To do so would be to impose on the Wanli Emperor, without even the awareness of insistence, our notions of childhood, freedom, and human formation, as if they were absolute, universal truths rather than the historical result in our culture of the post-revolutionary, romantic cult of the child. The Red Potter was not a twentieth-century child in emperor's clothes. He was a real emperor, the thirteenth of his family to be emperor, and he had always known, without misgivings or rebellion, that this would be his fate. Had the Chinese not had full confidence in his inner equanimity, had his understanding or confusion been an issue, had history not given examples of successful precedence, had the members of the court not conceived of ritualized peace as consonant not only with the emperor's identity but also with all their beings, had they modern notions of abstract justice or individual freedom, they would not have made him a child emperor, nor for that matter, made anyone else emperor.

But this leap to understanding is difficult for us, so that in these letters, the emperor is opaque and dim compared to Cervantes, who is our own bright image. Indeed, cultural misunderstanding seems frequent even among sinologists, so that information about China is often presented slant-eyed in the west, the great Samuel Beal, for example, saying in the introduction to his translation of seventh-century monk Xüan Zang's travel account, *Xi Yü Ji*, that normally "we think" of the Chinese as a "sluggish" people, or American diplomat Peter Townsend describing the Chinese, in *Ways That are Dark*, as the most despicable people in the world, liars and cheaters and devious grovelers, all.

While there may be Chinese who lie, Chinese do not like to think of themselves as a culture of deceivers; thus we try to imagine the emperor as he imagined himself, or at least as those around him saw him. There he is, wanly riding a black palfrey with white stockings in the imperial procession that is depicted on the long hand-scroll now owned by Wan-go Weng, the horse sprouting two long, golden pheasant-tail feathers that look like horns. He turns full facing outwards, showing a heavy, Buddha-like lower jaw, a prissy mouth, and beady eyes. He is lightly paunchy, though long of body, so that unlike the royal guards, ministers, and grand secretaries, or the two striding parasol bearers walking behind him, he looks unusually fleshy, even sluggish. His full-body armour with entwined dragons on each breast merges with the linked armour of his horse. His shoulder and arm plates are gold. His gold-rimmed bow scabbard is carried on his left side and shows a green dragon on a white field. In his bejeweled, delicate, white right hand, he brandishes a whip. His eyes are slightly rouged. His helmet, like those of his guards, is spiked and topped with tufts of red and white pennons. Though he carries a full scabbard, his arrow carrier follows with another, while a second bearer brings his western-style sword with its ivory and mother-of-pearl handle and sheath.

He is twenty-four years old—already showing signs

of a glandular condition that caused him dizzy spells and back and leg pains, and that, in twenty years, would bloat his body so enormously that he could not stand by himself, eventually killing him at the age of fifty-eight, dehydrated after two months of burning, raw diarrhea while his hands and feet swelled dropsically to watermelons—and he is on a visit to Ding Ling, where his underground tomb is being constructed, for, beginning with his attachment to his third wife Zheng, his intimations of death were so strong as to change his whole way of living. He forced the issue of his tomb construction against all attempts at censorship and criticism of the inauspicious nature of the rocky terrain, and shortly thereafter moved third wife Zheng and their beloved son Changxün to a small, wooden house behind the women's palace, where he lived a secluded and domestic life together with them. Slowly, during a long period of strange natural and unnatural disasters, some of which are described and analyzed in James W. Tong's *Disorder Under Heaven: Collective Violence in the Ming Dynasty*—disturbing astrological portents, earthquakes, typhoons, floods and droughts, violent uprisings, famine, the sudden appearance of red-bearded, long-footed evil-doers, *fou lan ji*, from heaven knows where—he withdrew from his general audiences with the grand secretaries who conducted the business of the empire, eventually cutting off all contact with the government for twenty-five years, making no decisions of state whatsoever, so that a whole generation of grand secretaries came and went without seeing him, for example Li Tingji, who was chief minister of state for five years without ever being in Beijing, and who tendered his resignation 120 times without answer, so that for a quarter of a century, the internal and external affairs of the empire stopped, and the Jesuit Alvaro Semedo wrote in his history of the reign that the emperor "never suffereth himself to be seen," and that "he is always shut up in a glasse, and only sheweth one foot, and such like things," somewhat distorting the popular Taoist explanation of the emperor's illness that he was made of glass.

Zhu Yijün's withdrawal from politics had enormous consequences in China's history. It is said (see Li Guangbi, *Ming chao shi lüe*; Xie Guoshen, *Ming Qing zhi ji dang she yün dong kao*; and Ray Huang, *1587, A Year of No Significance: The Ming Dynasty in Decline*) to have caused corruption, distrust, in-fighting, disloyalties, the growth of a crony-based power structure within the ranks of the emperor's personal eunuch attendants, grown by this point to some seventy thousand strong and operating as a unit apart from the headless government, and, ultimately, the total collapse of Chinese dynastic rule, which in turn led to the conquest of China by the Manchurians some twenty-four years after Wanli's death. Some historians say that the emperor's strangely reclusive and inattentive ways came from his opium habit; others point to a streak of madness in the family tree: his granduncle, Zhengde, neglected his duties and left the secluded city to carouse for weeks at a time, and, for a short period, wore sheepskin clothing, lived in a blue felt tent he set up in one of the courtyards, and ate roasted mutton from the point of his sword; his grandfather, Jiajing, abandoned state administration and became an alchemist; his diffident father, Longching, managed the state perfunctorily before dying young for no reason at all; and, of course, his mother became slowly demented during his mid-twenties and would wander around the royal woods north of the palace methodically tearing the leaves off the huckleberry bushes, which she said were taking over the hillside, working late into the night by the light of lanterns held by her attendants. But the Wanli Emperor's letters to Cervantes show him to be neither mad nor drug-addicted, but rather a man fixed to an awareness of his identity as emperor, who, as the final product of his whole culture at its historical apex, is given the impossible task of negotiating history's future with the heavens. Indeed, he was an ultimate emperor, and both his understanding and his dedication far surpassed those of his critics.

From the age of five, he spent every morning from dawn to midday studying the nine classical texts, *Sishu wujing*, in a yellow-tiled building on the east side of the secluded city, called the Garlands of Literature. Before dawn, the six ministers of state, the two censors, and all the grand secretaries of all the departments would gather in the courtyard of the Garlands to wait for him to take his seat inside on his Chair of Flowering. In the winter, they would shuffle and stamp silently, peering stupidly into the coals of the braziers, their backs turned towards the wind, their shoulders hunched beneath layers of camel hair and down padding. In summer, they would stamp the ground loudly, clearing their throats and remarking upon the songs of the birds in cages hung all around the courtyard. They entered the Garlands bowing, then prostrated themselves before finding their ranked places along the sides of the hall.

The first librarian unbinds one of the books of the four philosophers—the *Analects* of Confucius; Zang Shan's account of Confucian teachings, *The Great Learning*; Confucius's grandson Kung Ji's *Doctrine of the Mean*; or the *Works* of Mencius—and opens it to the textual citation for that day's lecture, laying it before the emperor on one of the low tables in front of him, while on a second table, he places the scroll on which is written that day's lecture interpreting the text, keeping it open with weights in the shape of carnelian dragons. Two men holding poles hung with lanterns illumine the tables with wavering circles of light. The Hanlin lecturer enters, prostrates, and then, facing the emperor, delivers his lecture, which reconstructs the etymological likelihood of the pictographic contents of the characters of the text, tracing the forms back historically to their shamanistic origins, or, running on the text like a John Donne sermon, following each figure or metaphor from its literal meaning upwards to its anagogic application. In any case, the lecturer's sole function is to bring the moral content of an ancient text into modern and actual signification and to demonstrate the means of interpreting and understanding these texts, which the Hanlin Academy investigated as its only duty.

If the emperor stares ahead vacantly or if he fidgets in his seat, the lecturer will stop, and one of the men holding the lantern poles that illuminate the lectern tables will lightly touch the emperor on his dragon cap with a paper lantern while an anonymous voice from the audience recites one of several passages from the Four Books that asks whether the emperor is above propriety. When the delivery is over, a second librarian approaches the lectern tables, removes the previous text, and replaces it with a passage from the *Spring and Autumn Annals* and its accompanying lecture. A second academician then enters the hall and delivers his course of instruction. In this way, the whole morning, every morning, is passed, the texts of the past made interesting and provoking, enlivened by ritual, made surreptitiously true by their placement within an ordered system whose legitimacy is simultaneously demonstrated and indoctrinated each time Shen Zong sees the officials line up in order of rank around the hall. All these things the academicians of the Hanlin would then discuss in the afternoon as they prepared the lectures for the next morning.

As a result, the emperor was superbly educated, even perhaps, since he carried on his course of study continuously for fifty years, better educated than any other man in the world. At the age of ten, he began composing examination questions for the *jin shi*, the highest degree in the national examinations for the civil service. Why was it, he asked at the age of eighteen, in a question written out by the anonymous *tung-wei* scribe as an essay of over five hundred characters, that the more he tightened governmental self-regulation, the more corruption and mistakes there were? Was this due to negligence regarding his personal morality, or because of administrative inefficiency, he wanted to know, and was there a reason that a reason could be given, he wondered. At the next examination, three years later, he asked for an explication of the Taoist notion that a good government could function without the emperor doing anything.

He was not only educated in political science, history, philosophy, and poetry, but, early on, he extended his sessions at the Garlands of Literature into geography, astronomy, music, medicine, mechanical arts, and natural sciences, and, after contact with Ricci, into the knowledge and languages of Europe. In the Garlands, he heard the polyphonic music composed by Barndoor Li performed on a harpsichord by I Follow Confused, who also taught him Spanish and gave daily readings from *Don Quixote* in that hall of learning; and he heard his cousin Zhu Zaiyü analyze this music in terms of trigrams based on a twelve-tone scale of equal temperament, calculated according to the twelfth root of the number two; and he heard Li Zhi defend the innate wisdom of the child in face of the world's multiplicity and change; he heard De Qing describe his out-of-body experiences and Zhenge explicate the eighty-eight names of the Buddha that form the meditations of the Chan; and it is here, in the Garlands, that he also heard lectures on the fifth-century discovery by Buddhist monks from Kashmir of the land of giant mulberry trees, called Fu Sang, which was located across the eastern sea on the northern Californian coast; and he heard of the coryneps, the whitish yellow larva of a Tibetan moth that is infected by the spores of a fungus, which grows a mycelium in the larva's intestines, thus killing it by consuming its flesh outwards until only a husk is left, out of the shell-like head of which grows a club mushroom with properties that will restore the human liver to balance when eaten daily; and he heard how to perfume his house with wooden panels of inlaid agaru and different tanwoods from Arabia—the yellow or red-brown sandalwood, or the light and brittle sand variety, called *chandana* by the Buddhists, which is derived from old trees when their bark is thin and their wood full of fragrance; and he heard accounts from merchant travelers of fishermen who go far out to sea in calm weather to fish with hooks the size of a man's arm, using a chicken or a duck as bait, and when they hook a big fish, the fish will pull the boat for half a day, and they will need another half a day to land it, and if the big fish is not good to eat, they will open it up and eat the little fish inside it, and inside those are littler fish yet, or if the weather is dark and rainy, the boat will go forward as she is carried by the wind, without any definite course, and in the darkness of the night, only great waves are to be seen, breaking on one another, emitting a brightness like that of green fire, with huge turtles and other monsters of the deep all about; and he heard of the analysis by his academicians of the bones brought by the Jesuits as a gift from the Pope that indicated such bones could not be from immortals, since an extrapolation of their makeup showed them to belong to beings that were far too heavy to fly.

Although he followed the path of inaction, Wanli was intellectually and emotionally energetic and curious. In the winter of 1600-1601, when the eunuch Ma Tang told him he had met some illegal foreigners dressed as mandarins who spoke a Nanjing dialect of Chinese and who were preaching Buddhism on the frozen Grand Canal, he immediately sent academic painters so as to depict them to show him what they looked like, and when he saw the portraits of Matteo Ricci and Diego de Pantoja and heard their comical names, Barndoor Li and I Follow Confused, he said, "Why, they're only *hui-hui*," meaning, according to the *tung-wei* scribe, that they must be Uighurs, and thus harmless, that their worthless presents of several golden clocks, a large wooden cross, some pieces of bones in metal boxes, some pictures of a woman and a forlorn man, a leather-bound book, and a box-like musical instrument, which turned out to be the harpsichord that he later enjoyed, were to be accepted, that they themselves were to be given permission to reside in Beijing and someday brought to him to explain how the clocks and the instrument worked. Of course, the scribe did not know that this off-hand remark, made in the aromatic sitting room of Wanli's small, private house, would be the most important decision the emperor ever made in his life, perhaps the most consequential decision any Chinese emperor ever made. It should be remarked that Shen Zong's identification of the Jesuits as *hui-hui*, which literally means "returned, returned," was less a mistake than an expression of clear understanding, for while Claudio Acquaviva and, indeed, all of Europe, thought Ricci was bringing Christianity to pagan China, China was already Christian, the Uighurs having been Christianized by the followers of the Patriarch Nestor of the Eastern Church as early as the sixth century (that is, at about the time the newly arrived barbarian tribes of Europe were being Christianized), the religion spreading to such an extent that during the twelfth, thirteenth, and fourteenth centuries, when China was ruled by the Mongolian Yüan dynasty, many of its rulers, ruling families, and members of the court and administration were Nestorian Christians. In his third letter to Cervantes, the emperor even argues that China had been Christianized directly by Christ himself. Years later, in 1607, Ricci himself was to get unsettling revelations of history when he met Ai Tian and other Jewish intellectuals who, in Beijing for the triennial national examinations, visited Ricci and described the antiquity of the Jewish settlements in China and the possibility that they could be the lost tribe.

Shen Zong's meeting with Ricci was as decisive for his own life as for that of the world. Ricci—a brilliant student of Clavius, thoroughly trained in both the Ptolomaic and the "new science" that Donne said had taken all coherence from the world; an Aristotelian scholar and an expert in Simonidean artificial memory, by means of which he could repeat any sequence of 400 characters forwards or backwards after hearing them only once; highly literate in classical Chinese (so much so that the great philosopher Li Zhi, who knew him well, said that Barndoor had so well absorbed the classical writings that he was superior to anyone he had ever met) and speaking three dialects of Chinese, as well as Latin, Portuguese, Italian, and Spanish—was able to explicate to Shen Zong the breadth and depth of western learning and culture in long, informal sessions winter and summer for the next nine years until Ricci's death in 1610, so that the two men became unique in their ability to mediate as well as meditate on the differences between the two cultures, and it is a tribute to the catholicity of both men that Wanli saw that difference in the context of *Don Quixote* rather than in terms of science and technology, as most cultural commentators have done. Ricci, too, owed a good deal to the Wanli Emperor regarding his own intellectual formation, though that subject is beyond our pale, including Ricci's defense of the policy of "accommodation"—the altering of Christian practices to conform to local cultures—and the subsequent legacy of that Jesuit position in the controversy of rites in the Catholic Church for the next hundred fifty years—thus informing at a distance Jacques de Guignes' argument, on linguistic grounds, that the Chinese were an Egyptian colony; influencing also Jean-François Foucquet (the companion of Hu, who was committed to the Charenton asylum with the Marquis de Sade), who worked twenty-five years trying to show that the ancient Chinese text *Yijing* prefigured the coming of Christ; and affecting, as well, Nicolas Trigault, that elegant gentleman in Chinese robes depicted by Rubens, who fell into a deep depression trying to demonstrate the Christianity of Confucian terminology to the Vatican and hanged himself in Hangzhou—a controversy they all eventually lost, leading to the Papal suppression of the Jesuit missions. All owed much to Wanli's notion that China, not Europe, was the original home of Christianity.

During this whole period, the Potter led a quiet, domestic life with third wife Zheng and their son Changxün and their daughter Shouning Gongju, conforming, he believed, to a ritual performance of society's basic family unit, even while knowing, especially after his son came to maturity, the scandal of it all. For years, he cleverly rebuffed all attempts to get him to declare the despised Changlo as his heir apparent, tree trunk of the realm, or to send Changxün out of the secluded city, since, traditionally, matured younger sons were a political threat to both the emperor and the emperor to be. Finally, in 1612, when Changxün was already twenty-five years old, he was made Prince of Fu and, to the great economic distress of the whole province of Henan, given 600,000 acres of land in Lo Yang, on which he constructed a palace shaped like a battle formation called, in ancient Arabic, *d'al-Hir wa-l-kummayn*, which, as the emperor read in Mas'udi's *Golden Fields*, had once been built in Baghdad by the great Abbasid Caliph Al Mutawakkil based on a story about a king of Hira of the Numanides dynasty that was told him by a courtesan.

Thereafter, with Changxün gone and Ricci dead, the emperor's interests turned inward, though he still read a great deal according to the daybooks of the scribe. In the summer of 1615, however, very close to the time Cervantes met with the Chinese priest, the fifth son of someone from Shandong named Zhang entered Changlo's palace at night carrying an acrobat's pole and beat several of the presumed heir's attendants before being subdued. He was said to be part of a conspiracy that involved a person whose name could not even be uttered nor that person's wife's name nor her family's. The emperor convened a state audience, the first in twenty-five years, at which he appeared, though he was already too heavy to walk, and, in a show of accord with Changlo, declared the fifth son of Zhang to be crazy and sentenced him to death. During the next five years until his death, he was too ill to do anything but think and listen to readings. On hearing Xü Xiake's writings about the holy mountains, he made a single excursion, which he describes in his third letter to Cervantes, to the sacred mountain of the north, Heng Shan, but by the time he returned with third wife Zheng, he was already suffering his final attack.

VIII.

THE LATE MING DYNASTY LITERATUS DONG QICHANG paints his soft and easy landscapes. He knew nothing of Cervantes or *Don Quixote*. His watery and broad brush strokes build up contrasting textures almost haphazardly in a spacious openness; random and meandering streaks run down hillsides like rivulets, making shadows and substance; his mountains and trees tilt in leisurely ways that give them rotundity; the leaves are little circles or dabbed blotches or whiffs of angled dashes, the foliage all lying on top of one another but distinct. He painted in the styles of many great painters of the past and wrote about the ineffable differences of their *qi yün sheng dong*, the six principles of painting. His running script and fluid cursive calligraphy were as sought after as his paintings, and his scholarly and critical writings are still standards. But as a civil servant, he seems to have been undistinguished, even though, as holder of the *jin shi* degree and a member of the Hanlin Academy, he was well placed. For a while, he was the tutor to the heir apparent, Zhu Changlo, but he resigned that and other academic posts in order to pursue his personal interest in painting and calligraphy. See James Cahill's chapter on Dong Qichang's paintings in *The Compelling Image* and the biographical article on him in A.F. Wright's and D. Twitchett's *Confucian Personalities*. Nevertheless, it is to Dong

Qichang's perseverance to civic duty in stooped old age—symbolized in a portrait of him reproduced by Paul Moss in his catalogue *Between Heaven and Earth*, which shows Dong just before his death in 1633, dressed in formal attire, fighting cranes emblazoned on his red-robed chest, waiting by the Cloud-Wreathed Gate to Heaven's Peace, waiting upon the dripping of the water clock that would signal an audience with the Emperor Si Zong—that we owe the present existence of the letters Wanli wrote Cervantes. At the time of Shen Zong's death, the veritable records of his reign were in disarray, darkly filling several buildings in the secluded city. The running Ming history that Chen Yübi compiled had ended with his tenure as grand secretary in 1597, and its documents, including the daybooks written by the anonymous *tung-wei* scribe, were simply stacked in windowless warehouses. At his ascension to the throne, Changlo called his former tutor to Beijing to direct the Court of Sacrificial Worship and thus to undertake the compilation of his father's papers. At Changlo's death only a month after his investiture (poisoned by red pills made from the menstrual discharge of adolescent girls with fine hair and high voices), Dong Qichang, then sixty-five years old, saw his official position become ambiguous, but he pursued his assigned task for ten more years at his own expense and presented Wanli's grandson, the Chongzhen Emperor, with three hundred volumes of finely written transcriptions of documents selected from the records, along with a forty-volume analysis of the political weaknesses of the Ming governmental system, a critique entirely ignored. Three of the four letters Shen Zong wrote Cervantes are found in Dong's compilation; the other, first letter, as I have said, is extant only in fragments. In the chaos at the end of the Ming dynasty, when the rebel Li Zizheng took Beijing, the eunuchs charged with the defense of the palace instead opened its gates to the man who, earlier that year, had captured the Prince of Fu's Flying Formation Palace in Loyang and killed Wanli's beloved son, Changxün. When the secluded city was stormed again a few months later by the Manchurians, who established the next dynastic empire, Dong's volumes suffered damage, but, except for a few elisions, his transcriptions of these letters were saved.

However, because of Dong's editing and compilation, the work of the anonymous *tung-wei* scribe has been covered over. Not having the original scripts, we cannot identify the scribe's hand, nor even tell if he was one person or several. If he were a single man, as I imagine him to be, he would have been a little older than Shen Zong, having begun at an early age the life-long task of recording Shen Zong's words and actions and perhaps even his thoughts, and continuing daily to do so for fifty years, thus participating in all of Shen Zong's life, private and public, and so would have been not only as well-informed and as educated as the emperor, but also as well-indoctrinated, as caught up in his thoughts, perceptions, daily duties, rituals, intrigues, tendernesses, angers, loves and hates and disappointments, fears, enthusiasms, beliefs, values, and judgments, but, knowing the emperor in some ways better than the emperor knew himself, or, for that matter, probably better than he knew himself, he would also have been, indeed was, the emperor's shadow self, an identical twin in consciousness, even the emperor's conscience, since, as the representative of history, he would have advised the emperor as to the historical consequence of his actions, how his actions and words would appear to the future. His knowledge and understanding made him the ideal omniscient narrator of Shen Zong's life, a role he seems to have adopted since, more than merely recording the emperor's words, parts of the letters to Cervantes are written in the third person or in an ambiguous mixture of voices, in whose muffle I hear, or prefer to hear, the scribe himself, even as I know that an argument can always be made that these narrative parts of the letters are the interpolations of Dong Qichang.

The *tung-wei* scribe wrote the first of Wanli's letters to Cervantes sometime after 1607, which is probably the earliest the emperor could have read *Don Quixote*, though it could have been as late as 1612, just before he wrote his second letter, which Dong Qichang groups with the unidentified miscellany of 1612. This second letter is addressed to Mi Hai, an appellation that would have been meaningless to Dong, as it has been for other historians for almost four centuries, because it is no Chinese name, the character for "Hai" being one usually used to designate an exclamation of astonishment, the whole name being somewhat the equivalent of "Rice, wow!" But coming to Dong's compilation from Cervantes's Dedication, we immediately recognize *Mi Hai* as a transliteration of *Miguel,* which, coupled with the internal evidence of the letter, assures us that this text indeed forms part of Wanli's correspondence with Cervantes. Clearly the emperor or the scribe invented this playful name in the comical mode of Cervantes himself, and, in the letter, they delight in telling Cervantes about his namesake Mi Fu, the great Sung dynasty calligrapher, painter, scholar, and eccentric, modeling him on Cervantes's character, the glass scholar.

Cervantes responded to both these letters, writing first in 1615, immediately after the messenger priest left Madrid, and then in April of the following year, when he was still finishing the prefatory matters of *Persiles* but knew he was dying from a dropsical condition brought on by diabetes. A Portuguese copy of his first letter exists in the Vatican repository of the files of the Inquisition of Goa. (For an account of these activities see Antonio Baiao's two volume *A Inquisicaõ de Goa*, where it forms part of a group of papers collected for the investigation of Franciscan accusations against the Jesuit mission in China that claim that terms used for God, the Holy Spirit, etc. were taken out of Chinese philosophy and thus paganized, that the flock was allowed to feast on fast days and work on Sundays, that the saints were presented wearing shoes in their paintings, and that the Wanli Emperor's calligraphy was being displayed in the chapel in Beijing.) The emperor is recorded as the addressee, but the translation, obviously, has no signature. Yet we recognize Cervantes's authorship by the discussion of poetics and by references to the writing of *Don Quixote*.

Cervantes's second letter, written on his death bed, is more certain, since I have the holograph in my personal collection, having bought it in Mexico City in 1980 from a rare book and manuscript dealer who did not recognize the hand. Being in the store to ask about sixteenth- and seventeenth-century Mexican emblem books, and finding the dealer quite ignorant on the subject, I had begun browsing disdainfully through a folio of miscellaneous manuscripts when, from a scholarly habit of focusing on the incomprehensible, I found myself deciphering the difficult handwriting of this letter and discovering what I thought were oddly philosophical speculations about life and death—odd in that letters more often speak about money or what one ate for breakfast. My curiosity aroused, I found the dealer at his paper-strewn desk in the back of the store and asked him what he knew about the letter, which he looked at briefly, commenting chauvinistically that the letter was Spanish and of not much interest to him because the Spanish, with their rolling, lisping accents, looked down on Mexicans, thinking they were all Indians and barbarians. He went on to tell me huffily that once in Seville, his landlady, learning that he was Mexican, had marveled that he spoke Spanish at all. I was able to take advantage of his mood and bought the letter very cheaply, and when I got home, I spent several hours making a list of the writer's personal handwriting peculiarities and abbreviations, with the aid of which I suddenly recognized the signature. In Figure 1, I reproduce the letter's final page, with Cervantes's signature clearly readable as "cerb(an)tes."

We have no direct evidence that Shen Zong received these two letters, which would have been in the imperial archives if they ever arrived in Beijing, since Dong Qichang, not being able to read them, or not thinking them of value if he could, did not include them in his compilation. I suspect that they did arrive—a Spanish version of the first and a Portuguese copy of the second (the Spanish original being in my possession). This assumes that Cervantes followed the Jesuits' practice of sending two copies by different routes. They must have arrived after Cervantes's death, the first probably in 1619 and the second in 1620, those being the years that, according to Dong's compilation, the *tung-wei* scribe, not knowing he was writing a dead man, penned his replies. The fate of the original versions of the emperor's two replies I do not know, but I sometimes fantasize that, with the publication of this correspondence, and knowing that copies of Wanli's letters may have reached Spain, a myopic and hunched-over scholar will one day recognize the *tung-wei* scribe's loose and curling hand in a stack of old papers at the Rastro in Madrid, the way Cervantes himself, so used to reading whatever scraps of writing came before his downcast eyes, discovered Cide Hamete Benengeli's manuscript of *Don Quixote* in a stall in Toledo.

Readers in today's world of electronic and instant communication may find a correspondence carried on by means of letters that took years to reach their addressees somewhat fantastical, but we must remember that historically, writing letters served a moral and civil function that emailing or telephoning or conversing face to face do not: that is, by delaying responses and allowing, thereby, reflection, the tempering of an over-excited response, consideration, judgment, and a considerable amount of self-directed and other-directed examination of both issues and psyches. Letter-writing belongs to a rational mode of communication that furthers introspection, the creation and the recreation of the self in its engagement with another consciousness. It preserves a civility that the more instant modes of communication eschew in favor of spontaneous emotions. Perhaps the rude sentiments and style of exchanges on the internet owe as much to its unreflective immediacy as to its anonymity, or perhaps, without reflection, the identity of the self cannot grow, so that the verbal violence of immediate repartee demonstrates an essential anonymity at the heart of the culture. As we move out of a letter-writing culture, we move into a more direct, immediate, and heated arena of communication. We also lose the kind of self-knowledge that the mediation of time allows us, so that we might expect ourselves to become gradually less wise. Western culture became philosophical only as a result of the invention of writing. In Plato's writings, we see the irony of Socrates transforming face-to-face communication, with all its problems of rhetoric, ego involvement, and passion, into a dialogistic mode of thought which, though still oral, causes communication to circle back on itself, making a space for reflection, and thus allowing Plato to create a written moral philosophy. That long, philosophical tradition, embedded in the temperance of written discourse for which letter-writing is an emblematic module, will not disappear because of electronic devices of direct communication, but it will be segregated, even more than previously, from the daily lives of average people, so that the already large split between the reflective and the active will widen into the gulf of misunderstanding.

IX

A CAUTIONARY WORD MUST BE SAID about my translations from the Chinese, because the Chinese language says what it means so differently from English and European languages that an accurate translation of this correspondence seems impossible. First, the basic unit of Chinese writing is the character, which is not a word, since the word is a grammatical concept: that is, the word exists only as an element of a larger construct and is defined by its function within that construct as a "part of speech," we say, indicating both its dependence on spoken language and its function as a part of something else; whereas the character, being less dependent on the spoken language, derives its meaning directly from the graphic signs that constitute it and does not go through utterances for its meaning, and thus means without participating in a grammatical structure. Thus, when characters are strung together, their relationship to each other is not dictated by a grammar, at least not a grammar in the way European languages have grammar, and so is oftentimes metaphorical rather than grammatical. Meaning in European languages comes in oral utterances, and too few people have discussed how, why, and when the utterance was cut up into words to explain that utterance's meaning. Since European writing is simply a phonetic transcription of the spoken language, we can see the tendency to do without the concept of separate words in former writing systems—for example, in Greek and Roman inscriptions, which run all the words together without breaks, or, even as late as in Columbus's time, in European handwriting that does not space out words. Chinese writing, not being phonetic, may not depend on the kind of meaning that utterances make, and so may be a very different kind of language from spoken language. It is graphic and visually symbolic, each character having a separate and unspoken meaning that is not a unit of something else.

Trying to distinguish between words and characters, the scholar Lin Yütang suggests that the character is more like a syllable, but in spite of the success of his dictionary, that clever hypothesis only pushes him further into the aberration of positing the dependency of written Chinese on spoken Chinese, for syllables are only the sound elements of words and cannot simply be accumulated in the way that characters can to make phrases of meanings. Not being words, characters in sequence do not function as grammatical elements in a grammatical structure; they are not grammatically tagged as parts of speech, as articles mark nouns and endings mark verbs in English; their relationships to each other are not quite grammatically definable. When two characters form a kind of adjective-noun combination, I cannot always tell which is modifying which, since most characters, when put into the western grammatical mode, are able to be different parts of speech in different situations. Those characters we insist are verbs nevertheless have no voice, mood, or tense. As a result, Chinese speakers learning English often have grammatical difficulties—mix up pronouns, genders, tenses, etc.—unable to think in the Cartesian, mechanistic form of western languages; in contrast, westerners learning Chinese find it easy to negotiate and exploit the ambiguities of the language: consider, for example, Matteo Ricci's invention of his Chinese name "Madou," which I have translated as "Barndoor," because *ma* means horse and *dou* is an opening of sorts. But the exact relationship between *ma* and *dou* is uncertain. The expression "dog opening" is colloquial for a gap-toothed person. Was Matteo missing his front teeth? I think not, and so I take the phrase literally, using *ma* as a modifier of *dou* to form an Italian *impresa* with all its implied self-referentiality. While I recognize that *ma* is simply an easy—the easiest and simplest—version of the initial sound of Ricci's Italian name and need not carry the meaning of horse, and although some historians write his name with a little jade sign in front of the horse, changing the meaning to "carnelian," I still hold to the horse reference in his name, because "Madou" contrasts deliberately with "Matai," the great horse, the Chinese version of the latinate name of his namesake, the evangelist. The *dou*, by its association with phrases suggesting error, gives his self-chosen name an aura of submission—humble Matt, not the great Matt, humble, Italian Matt. Further, the character *dou* implies that his name is an opening and thus clearly refers to the Book of St. Matthew, which "opens" the gospels of Christ. So *Madou* is he, Matteo, the humble workhorse, the door to China for evangelical Christianity and the door to Christ for the Chinese, but also an Italian intellectual with a taste for aristocratic wit and a Chinese literatus with a desire for *da-cheng,* the great synthesis. But here I have made him just a barndoor.

Because of its agrammaticality, Chinese is said to be strongly dependent on syntax for meaning, but even this generalization is confusing. We glibly demonstrate syntax by saying that "man bit dog" does not mean "dog bit man," but we don't deal with "man dog bit," which is completely ambiguous in writing, meaning that a man bit a dog, a dog bit a man, and further can mean that some humanoid dog or some canine human bit something viciously, or can even refer to some kind of special bit used to restrain dogs and people. In speech, the speaker can bend the phrase's intonation towards one meaning or another, but in writing, it is just very Chinese. Western scholars, whose languages habituate them to a precision of meaning not apparent in Chinese, often argue desperately over the meaning of Chinese phrases, not because of interpretive differences, but because of differing attributions of grammatical parts of speech to the characters in those phrases, as in the case of the controversy over *qi yün sheng dong*, a phrase central to traditional Chinese aesthetics. When I think how difficult it is to construct an English palindrome of any length, a kind of measure of the rigidity of English syntax, I am amazed that in the fourth century, a legendary Suhui embroidered in satin for her ne'er-do-well husband, Doutao, Matteo's *dou*, who was banished beyond the Great Wall, a *xüan ji tu* of 840 characters that could be read forwards or backwards.

Meaning in Chinese threads through the reading of characters by hints and innuendoes, that is, if the characters are readable at all, for a further difficulty of Chinese results from the complexity of the graphic forms of its characters, there being 214 root forms from which the characters are made rather than the twenty-some letters of western alphabets, so that the slightest graphic difference results in a totally different meaning, as if the slant used to cross a *t* in English could determine a word's meaning. Mi Fu says that calligraphers have never been able to read the characters they write, that it is all great theater. He was speaking of the difficult characters, but he might have added that because these characters are so complicated to write, ancient calligraphers invented abbreviations and standardized a way of writing called the grass script, whose flowing simplicity blurs all differences between characters, so that unless one knows what one is reading, one cannot read a text in this script. Westerners are often driven to distraction by this game, but Chinese have learned to deal with linguistic fluidity—though in a general tone of lassitude, which permeates their theoretical writings—by standardizing interpretation, so that all ancient texts achieve a kind of cultural understanding through commentaries that themselves become standardized, so that Chinese will use whole phrases, whole passages, and sometimes whole books as if they were a single word, because these, unlike an original combination of characters, have some fixed traditional meaning. Westerners criticize this practice as plagiarism, but it is no more thievery than using words, which all come to us pre-used. What Chinese write is not the individual creation of an author but the accumulated and standardized meanings of the traditional culture. Only by understanding this linguistic basis of cultural conservatism can we see how, in Europe in the late Renaissance, by creating a partible or atomistic and mechanistic universe of meaning, the invention of grammar and the dictionary destroyed traditional culture and made possible that individual freedom of mind that is so characteristic of the west and its science, economics, and politics.

But paradoxically, while the fixity of tradition counters the ambiguity of syntax in written Chinese, it also creates its own ambiguity: many phrases mean something completely other than what they say because of their association with a complex traditional story. Take, for example, the story of Wang Xizhi's wedding. Wang Xizhi was the greatest of all Chinese calligraphers in the sense that all calligraphers over the past sixteen hundred years have written in his tradition. As a young man, he was already famous throughout the Qin empire, and because of that, he was thought to be somewhat haughty and snobbish, though he was only reserved and meditative. On a warm and luxuriant summer day in the Yangzi River basin where he lived, a local potentate invited him and all the other eligible bachelors of the town to a social gathering to meet his beautiful and talented daughter, also a famous calligrapher. When some acquaintances came to pick Wang Xizhi up before the party, they found him lounging in bed in the cool eastern pavilion of his house. Not wanting to be disturbed, he told them to go on without him and that he would join them later, but he soon fell asleep and missed the party entirely, thus insulting the potentate with what appeared to be his oafish pride. However, as things turned out, Wang Xizhi was eventually introduced to the lord's daughter. They fell in accord with one another and were soon married. Thus, in Chinese, the son-in-law is called "eastern bed."

The sources of other allusions have been lost, as one might imagine. The term for Suhui's palindrome, for example, *xüan ji tu*, means a diagram of some complex astronomical clockwork, both the *xüan* and the *ji* referring to gears and fine jade or pearls. Whether this term is a fanciful metaphor for a turnabout or whether it derives from an ancient story, I do not know, but perhaps someone does. Classical literary Chinese is full of such derivations, which span the whole of Chinese history and mythology and literature, so that until this century, when Chinese writing was reformed to conform to spoken Chinese, only a completely well-educated scholar could read and write, though, I hasten to qualify, to read and write in that slippery, metaphoric, uncomprehending, self-doubting, guessing way that I describe above, for to read and write as an European does, immediately and with precision of reference and clarity of understanding, is impossible for a Chinese. In western terms, even Chinese cannot read Chinese. Thus, to translate this linguistic-cultural complex into the Cartesian forms of English is more than, as the Italians say, treachery: it is a total devastation, from whose still-warm ashes rises the new phoenix of the translation.

A Latin translation of one of Wanli's letters may very well exist in Joseph Wicki's *Documenta Indica: Monumenta Missionum Societatis Jesu, Missiones Orientales*, but we would never be able to recognize it.

X

ONE MIGHT SAY THAT MY PESSIMISTIC DESCRIPTION of the linguistic comprehension of the Chinese results simply from my personal defects, my grasp of the language having deteriorated over fifty years of expatriation to presbyopic fuzziness, a charge I cannot entirely deny, since I not only hear daily the Americanizations of my speech but recognize daily the brittle out-datedness of my natural idioms. I have analyzed the progressive artificiality of the writings of Ivan Bunin in exile and have studied Vladimir Nabokov's transformation of his language from the stylizations of émigré Russian to the formal freedoms of modernist English. Immigration is a blurred place where we squint to see anything at all, and in this era of deconstruction, I am aware of my "beholder's share" in the correspondence between Cervantes and the Wanli Emperor, a correspondence marked by a cultural and linguistic disjuncture much like immigration itself. Like the *tung-wei* scribe's voice, my own hoarse rattles sound in these letters.

But also their words echo in me, for I share with Cervantes and Shen Zong the experience of a demented mother, whom I seem enabled to watch at this moment out my second-floor study window. Her dimmed vision cannot see the arc of the log as it leaves her swinging arms, but she hears it crashing through the manzanita and rhododendron just a few feet in front of her with satisfaction, and, counting slowly in her head, she stands, feet apart and arms dangling, waiting for her heart to stop racing so that she can bend over again to pick up another log. I see her arms swing rhythmically again, clasped to the heavy log, back and forth, three times, four times, and then the log flies into the underbrush. She did this all day and eventually would get the two logs to the house. Then she would eat, even though she did not feel at all hungry, three o'clock already and not yet hungry, time really didn't matter much to her.

Thus, like the Red Potter and Cervantes, I too am obsessed with sanity and insanity, with foolishness and truth and confabulation, with mothers and sons, with time and reality, with the much that we want to say and the little that we can say and the strange things that we do say, with the shapes of death that they and I live for.

THE EMPEROR'S 1612
LETTER TO CERVANTES

DEAR MI HAI,

Changxün has left, and I am disconsolate. Yet my life
has not changed, nor has the world: each morning the
moist darkness along the paths to the Garlands smells
as still and nascent as every other morning, a stroke of
Huai Su's calligraphy still feels as gleeful, a stroke from
Mi Fu's brush still awes me into tears of wonderment,
my desire for my wife Zheng's touch, caressing and
hopeful, and for the taste of her inner flow, which shud-
ders through her body, has not slackened, my concen-
tration is great and my understanding increasing, and
I am not undone, though I am disconsolate.

When Changxün was three, I showed him a tricolor

Tang horse and had the scribe write the character for horse, with its long, arched neck, its flowing mane, its four feet flying, and said, *this is the meaning for horse,* which, listening without effort, he understood and thereafter was able to read and write. In the beginning was understanding, and understanding speaks. It was as simple and effortless as all beginnings, and Changxün was and is still a beginning for me, my speaking simply speaking, him listening simply listening, so that in this one-sided conversation with him, no history contaminates intentions. I think of Don Quixote arguing with Cardenio over the characters in *Amadis*, a scene in which mad Don Quixote plays the role of sanity against mad Cardenio's insanity, and yet their speeches entangle the ways in which their pasts and futures reflect one another—include Cardenio's later sane discussions with Don Quixote's insane ones; contrast the reasonable way in which Cardenio's history makes him a madman with the unreasonable way in which Don Quixote chooses to be mad; contrast the experiences Cardenio has undergone with the experiences Don Quixote has read about in books, though they are all, finally, stories in books; prefigure the ways in which Don Quixote, having heard Cardenio's story, imitates him and absorbs him into his storied being, since these speeches prefigure the ways in which Cardenio, having experienced Don Quixote, is later influenced into speaking Don Quixote's bookish style to the curate and the barber; contain, even, transformations of action, whereby the rhetoric and disguises the curate and barber had planned for Don Quixote are expended on Cardenio instead—the speeches between Don Quixote and Cardenio being so heavy with what is not said about how they reflect each other, how their lives entwine, who they are within themselves as distinct from who they are for each other, and thus how they came to be in your mind, that I am amazed they opened their mouths to speak at all. I feel this same weighty convolution with everyone I speak to, all the bureaucrats with their personal needs and their altruistic convictions, all the eunuchs with their infamous squabbles, the scribe who listens with the ears of all those yet to be born, wife Zheng, whose feelings for her family harmonize all she hears, and my mother, with her understandable aberrations. But to Changxün I can speak simply.

Even that doubt I feel about myself speaking falls away when I speak to him, for normally when I speak, I think or feel or sense or have a certitude or just simply presume that I mean something—that I am consonant with my intention, that I have something to say, that there is a mindful cause for my speaking—even as I am haunted at once by the thought, the feeling, the sense, or the simple awareness that what I say may distort or not be what I mean, even as I listen to myself and wonder at how my words do not express what I mean.

Much as I know that my words are not my thoughts, yet, with the very impetus to speak, at the very moment of speech, I am filled with the aura of consonance between language and mind, for how else can speech arise in our throats? The heart supports sound to make meaning: I write *xin* under *yin* to form *yi*, heart under sound to show that language has meaning, sentiment, intention. So, as I speak, I am at a privileged moment when, before what I mean has vanished into the labyrinth of memory, I can hear at the same time what I desire to say and what I say, and thus I am able truly to say, *no, no, that is not what I mean, that is not it at all.* A moment later, that purity is lost. I am thrown again into a world of masks and ego and hypotheses and judgments about myself, for after that moment of privilege, my "no, that is not what I meant" means that I am in the throes of a revision and thus not consonant with my own vision, such that, correcting myself because I have over-spoken or have said something unconsidered or that needs qualification, as I am now doing, my assertion of the heart sound experience of speech has already been undermined by memories of the wormy deviations of us men.

What happens when I lie? Or, you, Mi Hai, what happens when you speak for the quiet Don? Are you truly yourself when you speak for him? I see that language's heart sound is a great problem, for we listen and we read always assuming that the words are informed by heart sound, but they do not have to be. Words are an empty palace we are born into, the halls and corridors of which, nooks and crannies, windows and doorways, were long ago constructed by innumerable and unknown builders and planners and workmen whose unknown and unknowable intentions and meanings are set in stone and wood and whose spaces form our whole lives, while we live so conformed under the illusion that we are ever building the palace the way we want it. The spaces of this palace may not even be anyone's intention, but only the result of an accident— for example, that there was more timber of one size than another available when a room was projected, or that some order from one person to another was misunderstood, or that a fire or earthquake destroyed parts of the edifice. Yet, in spite of all this, I am claiming that I intend what I speak, verifying heart sound as if I had made up that word, though I still cannot speak without that feeling that my desire flows effortlessly into speech. But with Changxün, it was no illusion. To him alone I spoke my intentions and he understood them. Now, without him, I am bereft of heart speech.

But if an emperor cannot say what he means, who can? In four hundred years, a Chinese scholar living amongst the mulberry trees of Fu Sang, east of the land where the sun is rooted, may pause when studying the emperor's speech and think that, not being the emperor of China, he himself could never speak, with the relief and calm of a deep breath held and suddenly released, the truths and convictions he had so long envisioned, fathomed, formed, studied and tested, truths about time and memory, wisdom and power, multiplicity and agreement, history, self, mind, language, form, culture, thought, knowledge, understanding, and truth. He would never be able to tell the truth of what he thought, because what he thought would have to be said as if it were understood as he understood it in the telling, as if he were speaking to himself, so that speaking was redundant with understanding, and only an emperor's speech, he might think, could be so unique. He wants to explain his daughter's fear of the dark as a second fright, not an ancient, original, genetic fear inhering in the human species, but an artificial fear created by a series of human inventions and ideas whose motivation was, first, a delight in natural conflagration, and subsequently the assertion of the individual egos of discoverers and inventors of fire and torches, lamps, candles, lanterns, and later still, the physical and moral gains of merchants who made new fuels and new forms of light, and whose incorporated successes in a capitalistic system created his culture's need, and thus his daughter's need as well, for perpetual incandescence, for a world in which all objects were always illumined, as if eyes had grown so weak that the sun's power had to be made to cling to things so they could be seen, as if the uncertainty of existence could be held in check by the radical presence of a lit world, leaving his generation, and thus him, the first in the world unable to walk the dark mountain paths of Li Po without what he took to be a man-made, historical, and not natural discomfort, an example of the artificiality of feelings and needs. But he fears that, having said this, these musings could be put on a shelf, an artifact, ignored as a nice but trivial idea, that they could be heard without realizing they were a description of a winter walk at night taken ten years earlier in Louisiana pine woods with his young daughter, a memory not of a thought, but of an image palpitated along its silent seams—a white feather fan, falling petals, a blue cloud—until it imparted its convoluted secret cultural determination. How grammatical European languages and how agrammatical Chinese, as if the European was always riding westward while looking east and the Chinese lying still and helpless at his own front door.

If he were to fill in all the interstices of his cultural history, unravel and stitch again the texts and contexts of his speaking, laying on one side the poetry of that fitful crisis, four hundred years earlier, of European culture called, perhaps, a renaissance, another birth, and so uncovering swirls of time, of memory and forgetfulness (forgetting begets memory begets time), since what is remembered must first be forgotten, laying too on that side the grammar of enlightenment, of science, of discovery, forwards and backwards, of law and circuitry, which made darkness glow with man-made sunshine, and then if he were to place on the other side Li Po's poetry—careless, tense-less, grammarless, without forgetfulness and so without memory, timeless, a culture of perpetual recording and an overwhelming present, a living in darkness—he could still convince no one of the absolute schism between these two diverging histories, would still be subject to accusation, charged with a totalitarian claim to a monopoly on truth, though he deny it, called an ideologue, an intellectual authoritarian, a cultural tyrant, undemocratic, which he would also deny, blind to both the evils of conviction and the wonders of disbelief. What he desires most—to speak his thoughts cleanly, as if in a monologue—would require breaking into dialogue, unless he could speak as *vates* or as poet, or, he might consider, as the great ancestor, the pathway to heaven, the gate, the foundation—superior, worthiest, highest, benevolent, righteous, war-like, refined, good, successful, and exalted emperor—as I.

In his imagination, then, as the Wanli Emperor, he stands on top a large, emerald prominence overlooking the invisible north sea and thinks of the chiastic phrase that he had deciphered that morning, *yo sé quién soy,* I know who I am. The bare outlines of buildings shift as billows of yellow sand swirl across their dim and ghostly forms. The masses waver and roll at times, at times drift slowly, yet at times their rectilinear shapes seem unperturbed, though with the pallid fixity of a painting, background to the energetic drama of yellow earth, whose wild rhythms he so eerily feels in his body as fierce buffetings. If he does not strain to see, nothing is seen but the varying thicknesses and intensities of earth covering the layers of upcurving, wing-like waves of gilded, tiled roofs, their blue and green ceramic inserts, the labyrinthine struts and gates and partitions and palisades of the pavilions and temples that dot the now rippled pine and bamboo hillside. The sea has disappeared entirely, as have the brilliant clay slants of the immense walls to the south. The island floats in the earthen sky. When he turns away from the wind, his face is a yellow mask, powdered like an actor's, his whisky beard and slightly bulging eyebrows, his prominent cheeks, his hanging jowls, all blending together in a sculpture of silt. He is not the wind, as Kong Fuzi said, nor is the wind that blows in the palace different from the wind in the city, as Song Yü told Xiang. So he is not amused or interested or even observant of the equally dusted faces of his eight immortals entourage as he squats to allow the carriers to lift him onto the palanquin for the descent, which winds along turquoise paths. He pulls the curtains closed.

A man is who he is, am I not who I am, the emperor thinks, for I can no more imagine myself my mother than I can imagine who I would be if I were your son, and since we are not only who we are, but who we are is limited by our imagination—such that, underneath all our uncertainties about everything, I at least have certainty that I am I—so he wonders why you could not say, or what it was that you meant not to say, about who the man is whose story you tell, pretending that you don't want to remember, and why wouldn't you want to remember, that you don't know, or that no one knows, whether his name is Quijada or Quesada or Quejana, or why he should become Quixote, or is it Quijote, if he is indeed who you say he is, and, thinking that, perhaps, his query might engender a response that, however sincere and serious, would distort or even set aside what he wants to know about this alien author. He wonders if perhaps the certainty he feels in his being were not the certainty of the son of heaven, wonders if mere man would feel the same am-ness, if, indeed, what your prevarication is, is not the yellow desert sand gusting into man's soul. That image gusts against his thought, shaking him. Even in the safest cranny of his knowing, he is himself, but to say who he is is fearful and uncertain, as if he could be sure that he *is*, though unsure of *who* he is, for to be any specific someone, even himself, denies being someone else, divides forever the total embrace of the heaven of his certainty, fortifies his *me* in impenetrable, permanent, giant red enclosures, segregating me from thee, me from all you others, an image of heaven, though not itself heaven, an image reflected in every city wall in the central empire. So this author from the country of liars was right after all not to say who the knight was, who his parents were, what village he lived in, for even though that knight knew he was he, he could not have but felt a loss of his wholeness were he to say who he was, except in madness. And, not having to say who Quixote was, you could imagine yourself him, demented and not yourself.

So even as this anonymous scholar of Fu Sang, whose father may have named him Wei for the fire-red color of my scribe's brush, a literary name, wants desperately to imagine—when he tries to imagine me—that the emperor alone can speak the truth, his own sense of impediment becomes more and more mine, so that his emperor ends up unable to say who he is, yet he is wrong. I have spoken without barriers. I have done so with my son, and thus I am disconsolate at the closing of the palanquin curtains.

But if Wei cannot imagine the emperor, can the emperor ever imagine him, in his plain humanity, a sliver of red earth, as he asks himself, perhaps, can the emperor ever know the truth? The emperor is surrounded by toadeaters and frivolities, and even his speech is taken from others. The closing of the palanquin curtains comes from a nonsensical poem told the emperor the previous week. The emperor, disputing with his chief eunuch over the interpretation of the passage *wen xin diao long* in the ancient Book of Odes, had sent for the poet Ni Hongbao, author of the emperor's favorite lines *(I grow old and mad for no reason / but a tall man is not necessarily better than a dwarf)*, who, after a long illness and convalescence, finally arrives at the emperor's secluded city one evening, where he is received with great courtesy, even though the emperor is drunk amidst his courtiers. When asked about his long voyage, Ni Hongbao said that while passing through the region Nu-ma-ni-ya, between Huai and Meng, he'd heard that a hospital for the insane was being established nearby, and, desiring to see what kind of people were considered insane, he, accompanied by a refined and well-read young man he had met on the trip, visited the place, where he found patients sitting and standing quietly among the potted plants and pathways of a large courtyard. Near the hospital's entrance, they encountered a disheveled young man who was standing by himself and to whom they spoke, inquiring as to who he was and why he was there. The insane man looked down at the ground for some seconds and then, looking up, began to recite a love poem—*flames of despair purify my heart, / I clasp my breast and fold into myself like a withered and dried flower, / alas, poor heart, alas, poor body, / my sadness doubles and my death comes soon after*—and so on. Ni Hongbao said the poems had so moved his companion that he began to recite love poems in return, and the two young men exchanged laments and complaints and tears until the patient began reciting a lament of separation: *They are gone / The palanquin curtains have closed / How did it happen? / Nothing frightens me so much as that lengthening distance / The camels rose to their feet and carried them off.* At that, Ni Hongbao's companion cried out, "They are dead." The insane man stopped and whispered, "Then so am I," and fell dead. Ni Hongbao waited until the man's body had been washed and wound in a sheet, then recited funerary prayers and had the patient, who was a Musulman, cremated. When Ni Hongbao finished his story, the emperor, who all the while had been reclining on a bed in a stupor, waved him to the side, the question about which he had been summoned apparently forgotten.

Then the poet Pu Tuyi, who was standing next to Han Ba in front of the emperor's bed, began to recite a long, sycophantic, laudatory poem that rhymed on the emperor's names and began *the mouth that smiles, the look that sears* and so on, then went on about beauty, bounty, justice, glory, light, and salvation, like the poems at the beginning of *Don Quixote.* At the end of the poem, he bowed demurely and began backing up with his head bent, but Han Ba leapt forward from his place and asked the emperor to bring the poet back to hear his parody, which, being done, allowed Han Ba to begin rolling out nasty anecdotes and calumnies about Pu Tuyi begging for favors and eating out of people's hands. Before he'd finished, the emperor was laughing so wildly he'd rolled off his bed. He ordered that a thousand yüan be given to Han Ba, and when his eunuch Ao Fa reminded him that Pu Tuyi had been the butt of Han Ba's jokes, the emperor had a thousand yüan given him also, and, remembering Ni Hongbao, this nothingness we had brought from his home, gave him a thousand yüan, too. Then the emperor, now much awakened, asked Han Ba to tell the story of his donkey, which Han Ba did by elaborating on the virtues of his dead donkey, the most sensible ass in the whole herd, never stubborn, always sure-footed, though a sudden illness had spirited him away, but then the ass appeared to him in a dream. "O, my dear ass," he said to the donkey, "what happened to you, didn't I take the best care of you possible, was not your water fresh, your straw most carefully bedded, how did you die," and the donkey answered that one day, when Han Ba had stopped by the herbalist to talk about a fine shipment of yellow Tibetan worms, a splendid assess had passed by, and seeing her, his heart had been taken, he loved her with a love so passionate that he'd succumbed to sadness and despair. Han Ba asked his ass-ghost what poetry he had composed about all this, and the ass responded, reciting: *My heart was taken by an assess, / in front a dry-goods store, / enslaved by gentillesse and by her smile, an enchanting bower, / by her prance so full of finesse, her cheeks as fresh as a flower, / to live would be a weakness, so I died from love dishowor.* When Han Ba asked what the word "dishowor" meant, he was told it was a rare word in the language of asses. The now-cheerful emperor ordered his musicians and singers to set the ass's poem to song and showered Han Ba with presents.

No, the emperor never knows the truth. I am told that a thousand a day die of cold in Beijing in the winter, and I order the warehouses to be filled with rabbit skins so the homeless may burrow in them to keep warm, but all winter long I hear reports of the fires that the beggars have lit in the streets, and I do not know why they have not gone to the warehouses. Not knowing the truth, not being able to speak the truth, can I condemn drunkenness and frivolity, for everything I know, like everything Don Quixote knows, comes from a story, and perhaps the report from Ni Hongbao to the court was only a story to amuse me? North of the Yellow River, in the Province of the Eastern Mountains, the people suffer unending famine, drought, earthquakes, floods, repeated devastations by locusts and bandits. When I was fifteen, I was told that during a recent famine, the peasant farmers in one of the southern counties, perhaps the riparian county of Tanzheng, managed to stay alive by selling their lands at prices far below their worth to speculators who took advantage of their misfortune, but without their land, farmers could only beg, so I invalidated all the deeds of purchase, declaring the sales unfair because of the sad constraint upon the farmers. A few years later, another famine occurred in a neighboring county, but this time, the sharks were wary of coming near, and thousands of people starved to death because they could not find purchasers for their lands. The emperor cannot know the truth. It is no wonder my countenance is sad.

Gods may cavort and fight and swoop down upon nubile young women with lightly erect breasts, brushing them with their immortality, but the sky is simply supreme and absolute and beyond conception, broad in all directions, present and everywhere at all times. Everything that happens happens under the sky; even the doings of gods and ancestors cannot escape its presence. The earthly causes of happenings, all the accidents of life, all the willed actions of people—doltish Liu castrating himself, sending me his gonads in a purple, silk-covered box and chaining himself to a rock outside my house for nine years because he had a dream in which he violated my mother; all the growing of trees and sorghum and millet and rice and cabbages and the maize, sweet potatoes, and peanuts that I brought from New Spain; the curdling and rotting of tofu into cheese; all the infestations of lice and locusts, all the storms, sands blowing, the heat of summer—all these happen under the sky, with the sky, not because of the sky, for the sky has no will, no intention, no cause, but is itself, in its mystery of being, like the overseer of the complexities of existence. It has nothing—is nothing—but being itself.

I am that same presence on earth. I am the son of sky. Just as we all need names to use in our place as symbols for ourselves, so the sky needs a symbol to protect its absoluteness. Sky has no life, and I am a living symbol. I am the sky's living representative. When a farmer in Suzhou has been cheated by speculators who befriended his daughters and gave the old man drink so that he signed away his land, he can come to my city gates and revile me for letting such a thing happen. When the Yellow River overflows its banks every spring, the people can feel satisfaction by complaining to my Board of Water Control and my Board of Rituals. If the people suffer exceedingly, they can kill me and feel justified that they have done something to better their lives. They can revile me, hurt me, and be assured that their actions have some effect on me, for I am hurt, I suffer, I can be killed. To the sky, they can do nothing, and that imperviousness is too much for people. It seems to them indifference. It makes them feel ineffective, unable to act, not themselves. They need to complain. They need to punish. In the same way, people need to be able to give me pleasure, to praise me and worship me and know that I enjoy their offerings when they are happy. In this way, the sky is brought into daily life, into every act of thinking and feeling, into soul and consciousness, into the very psyche and selfhood of everyone. I make life bearable for everyone, for life, in fact, is too difficult, too bewildering, too tragic, too comic, too complicated, and too always changing, too, to live directly. But you see now I cannot judge anybody—least of all the emperor, who drinks away his hours listening to frivolous love stories about asses without the slightest understanding of love—cannot disgrace him for being what he is. It is enough, more than enough, that I know about him, and that I doubt what I know. That is my only occupation in life, to know everything and to hold that knowledge in still balance against my ignorance of everything, so that between curiosity and suspicion, everything can occur. It is not a job akin to traveling from village to village collecting wheat for the king's army, which is only a technique of survival, nor is it like being a low-ranking court official, which is the courtesy or polite behavior of someone who has passed the state examination, nor like being a poet, which is the pleasure of literacy. My living is not a job, but something that I must do to play my role in life. Only the peasant is like me, playing the role of earth in life, bound to the earth's changes, growth, and disasters, symbol of the receptive. Every day till every darkening of the day, I lie propped amid cushions specially constructed because of my gout, either outside in one of the pavilions of one of the gardens or inside my private chambers, where I read or listen to memos such as the one I've related to you so that I can know everything that happens under the sky. I do not step into the Golden Heaven Audience

Chamber or sit on the Dragon Throne raised by three tiers of earthly squares where, before me, my father and the other emperors listened to the arguments of their councilors, advisors, and ministers on the making of the policies, judgments, laws, and regulations according to which the land is governed; I long ago realized that this was not my purpose as the sky's representative, for the sky does not govern, does not judge, but allows all to pass, everything.

With Changxün, I would talk of these things, or so I now think I did, but perhaps I only felt so close to him—so much a part of his being a person that I felt he was a part of mine, felt he participated so much in my being that we seemed to discuss everything—when in fact I said nothing. Only the scribe knows what I said, and he does not tell me, for he writes only to be read in the future, by Wei the scholar in the tall mulberry trees. I might have explained that while Han Ba's silly poem corrects the overly serious Persian love stories of tattered, mad lovers streaking through the woods— vignettes of instant love and instant death—and so may be preferable to Ni Hongbao's story of the mad lover, yet Ni Hongbao is no fool, for he recalled to me the origins of the love story's platitudes, which were once attacks on propriety, on the listless imagination unstirred by sentiment, blind in its own darkness, unelevated by the unexpected. Love's narration of excess, madness, and unpredictability rebukes those public hypocrites with dullard faces who always call for decorum and piety and right behavior—they do not stand in the wind with me—those who criticize my pleasure, memorialize me for my inaction, who forced me to send Changxün away. And even if these attacks have now themselves become platitudes, that very commonness that Han Ba mocks, have become incorporated into the constrained life, still their clichés propose, no matter how weakly, multiplicity, chance, and the unexpected. So, knowing my love for Changxün, Ni Hongbao told me a story that is not without irony, and the closing of the curtains is not without meaning. Such stories are rituals of surprise. Mi Fu bowed to grotesque stones, called them brothers, and was a great painter. Perhaps I told Changxün the story of Chen Jiru.

Chen Jiru, having been turned down by the Wanli Emperor for a job as royal tutor because of his disreputable looks, was on his way back to Jiangsu when he met the famous general Chi Yüanjing, who gave him a lift on his boat down the Grand Canal. On board, the general regaled Chen Jiru with stories about his battles against Japanese pirates on the north coast, how he developed special long weapons to nullify Japanese swordsmanship, and the unusual formations his volunteer troops were trained in, demonstrating these maneuvers with large movements of his arms and bellowing sound effects. In one story, he told how he was visited on the eve of a battle by the ghost of General Wang Jian of the Qin, who bantered with him over a cup of wine, saying that if he were alive, he would show Chi Yüanjing the proper understanding of Sun-zi, but Chi Yüanjing responded by saying that were Wang Jian alive today, even his lieutenants would be able to out-maneuver him. At the end of the evening, General Wang Jian wrote in the sand a strategy for the next day's battle. The next day, Chi Yüanjing followed the ghost's advice—not to fight until the rains came down so heavily that the Japanese began to retreat—and he won the battle. Chi Yüanjing was pleased with his story and unrolled a scroll to show Chen Jiru his copy of what the ghost had written in the sand. Then he had a curtain hung and they were entertained by a beautiful young lute player and a moon-faced guitarist who sang love songs back and forth until the girl playing the guitar sang, "Pity for lovers who are cruelly separated," and the lutenist answered, "What should they do?" The girl with a face like a brilliant moon replied, "This is what they do," and, tearing away the curtain, leapt into the water, whereupon a handsome page dropped the white feather fan he'd been holding, cried out, "Fate decreed that it be you," and jumped in after her, both perishing in each other's arms, though the sailors tried to turn the boat around to save them.

Intensity loses itself in its own excess, but the ritual of the torn curtain remains a figure for the suddenness of life. Even when insipid, poetry is much wider than the sanctities of right behaviour, so there must be room for Pu Tuyi's sad, whining poem of praise, which hides his self-respect while begging for alms, just as there must be room and value also for the buffooneries of Han Ba under my sky. What matters, under the sky, is only that there be stories, that, like life, they go on and on, interrupting each other, losing themselves in interruptions, picking up again and going on, new ones arising in the midst of others, stories branching and rooting or fading imperceptibly into yet other stories.

My aim is to think the thoughts of others, to feel the feelings of others, not so much to do what others do as to know how to do them, not to whistle or sing or climb or make money or vitrify *bai dunzi* into porcelain or chant the eighty-eight names of Nien Fo, but to know and experience what it is like to do these things, purely to teach myself to perceive and to articulate those thoughts that others express but that I have never before thought, to learn how to have these intelligences and poetries and feelings and perceptions, until I am able to conceive, give birth to and to perceive, to make flesh, as you *hsi-yang* people say, a world populated, to see from every angle, to relate to every existence, to hear all the puns in all the languages, to realize all the metaphors for our feelings, to understand all the references, and to interpret the world as the world, as everyman under the sky. Perhaps we are not so different, for is that not the kind of writer you are willy-nilly creating for your world? And I imagine that your function in life is very much like mine, to provide the people of the world a sense of themselves, so that above and beyond the values of the world, people, whatever they do under the sky, when they see themselves in your stories, will know that they have value in the eyes of the writer. So reading about the most extreme passions and actions in the most extreme circumstances, as well as the daily and boring lives of commonplace people, comforts. Perhaps this is the reason, before I was able to say why, I sent for you to teach at the Hanlin Academy, though I found so much of your work plain when I first read it.

The litter bearers slowly carry the emperor down the emerald prominence, led by firefly lanterns and fifers whose melodic tendrils drop in tattered bits out of the blowing dust. The eight immortals follow behind, though their robed shapes can hardly be seen. As the cortège winds through the pine woods at the bottom of the hill near the eastern sea, it passes the attendants of the August Empress Dowager Cisheng, whose lanterns light up her strange form standing in the undergrowth. Protected from the buffetings of the wind by the rhododendron and huckleberry, she stands tottering on her tiny, bound feet, her arms at her sides, resting. She wears the blue blouse and pants of a workman. The emperor's palanquin does not stop, and as the litter passes the assembled attendants, he hears the crashing of the log his mother heaves through the brush. She will do this until she reaches the jade boat pavilion by the sea's edge, braced sidewise to the direction of the throw, swinging the log in her hands back and forth across her body, once, twice, three times, then releasing, then resting in the lantern light while her attendants clear a path to where the log has fallen.

If Changxün is the only person to whom I can speak, was I thus for my father, whom I remember only as colored silk cloths floating in the air and then as the terrible drip of the melting ice by which his body was kept fresh? I cowered in the dark corner of the hot and perfumed room, left there during the nightlong prayer for the dead as the drops of water struck the floor irregularly below his bier, fearful not of him nor of death, but of that dripping, the beats coming sometimes almost on top of one another, then the interval lengthening out as if silence had at last prevailed, yet always there again, drop, drip, drip, drip, drop. I remember nothing else.

With my mother, I remember everything, but she remembers nothing, so I will never know if she spoke to me uniquely, as if to herself, who no longer knows who I am nor who she is, though, strangely, she is still who she has always been. Indeed, it may be that by having forgotten everything, she is now able to always speak directly and clearly, for without *if*, without *when*, without *I hope,* without *I fear,* without *want* or *must* or *would that I could* or *ought to,* her characters play out their scenes in her head flooded by the direct light of the present active, out of all time, like Chinese, without tenses, unfiltered by any subjunctive sense of self-conscious duality, so that whatever she thinks is objective, existent, and thus true, as little concerned with her as the fir trees around her house that always seem to her to have sprung up overnight, piercing the sky overhead with their rigid gestures of growth, and that are so clearly not of her making that they could thus hardly be doubted without irritating her. Unable to come to terms with either what she thinks or feels or imagines, or what she sees or hears or smells, she forgets nothing, has nothing to forget, and remembers nothing. Time has lifted its heavy fingers off her sensibility, and she floats through space without any motivation or need. She stands in the midst of the woods, still and unmoving, for hours at a time, or she stands staring into the darkened mirror of her bedchamber, her arms folded across her chest, until the lantern bearer's entry forces her to go somewhere else to escape his necessity. What images arise in her mind become increasingly flattened, not only stripped of all locative markers, unplaceable in time's dark tunnel, but so fixed that they do not change in the slightest way through being recalled and forgotten and recalled again, each appearance indistinguishable from its previous emanations, because each occurrence is the same occurrence. Though death has not stopped for her, she has stopped for death. Freed from the hesitancies of time and self, she can truly be who she has always been. "Hai," she said to me one morning after three days of arguments over her dimming sight, which she refused to accept, "I know now that my eyes cannot deteriorate, because I don't have any, having exchanged them years ago, I just remembered, for glass eyes, and glass cannot deteriorate."

When Changxün was young, I took him to visit her at the Ci Ning palace, thinking that she, who was so good at elephant chess and *wei qi,* could teach him, and that this preoccupation in time and mind would ward off the fantasies of her monkey mind. "No, no, I don't remember how to play," she'd objected, but when the board was laid out, her hawk-like hands seized the pieces unhesitatingly, *Ha, I'm taking that piece, ha, that elephant is dead, ha, I'll take that one, ha, mate,* and she knocked Changxün's emperor over and over again, mate and again mate, with such delight, her pleasure no longer disguised as a lesson, as had been the case with me, *Oh, he will learn on his own, which is the best way.* I watched Changxün's silence as if it were a piece of gauzy, wet silk laid over an embankment, the dark and light spots suggesting a landscape of my youth that I had never before entered. I did not realize that I had been unhappy as a child, always defeated by her, frustrated and straining to overcome the weighty superiority of her stratagems until I was fourteen, when I finally beat her in chess and thereafter refused to play, which is why I was unable to teach Changxün.

She might have planned all this, intuiting the distant effects of her pedagogy of self-sufficiency much as she unerringly and immediately saw the spatial configurations of the checkered board, which transforms itself continually into changing positions of power and weakness, might have planned for me this life I now lead, planned for me to bring Changxün to the Ci Ning palace for spiritual exercises of strength. But if so, she has forgotten it all, even as her intent unrolls itself as my life. Now that consciousness has fallen away, only pleasure is left, the simple joy in winning. This, it seems, is who she really was and is. She comes from a lowly military family, her conniving father having been demoted and reprimanded repeatedly for selling military requisitions on the black market, and she was only a maidservant in the female quarters when I was born. I always thought her great climb resulted from sharp ambition, but now that she resides outside time, I see that inside herself she has always played for the pleasure of winning, whether or not that joy lifted her up in the status of men did not matter so much.

As she reveals herself in her madness, I seem to know her better and better. In her insanity, she happily leaves red ribbons tied in bows pinned to the walls or dangling from the lanterns by her bed. I see her humming to herself as she methodically and haltingly ties the loops with her arthritic fingers, something she would never have done in her hard, rational life, and though this childish concern for prettiness is so unlike who she has been, her fancied pleasure is so obviously herself that it saddens me, a maudlin pity, layered, however, by a shock of recognition, and perhaps of self-recognition, since revelation is a gusty wind that shakes the whole tree. But revelation is also never reciprocal. The more she reveals of herself, the less is she able to know me. The more I am the watcher, the less I am watched. And this imbalance may be true between Changxün and myself as well. The more clearly I spoke to him, the less did I hear him speak. And, for his part, the more he listened, the less he understood, so he may only know me when I am lost and grown silent, when I can no longer know him. Thus I am triply bereft by his leaving: nevermore to speak cleanly, nevermore to hope to hear him, nevermore the chance to be known.

So be it.

I.

CERVANTES'S 1615
LETTER TO THE EMPEROR

To the Emperor of Ming, Red Clay, Great Potter,
Ancestor, Roots, Shining, Broad, Son of Heaven,

Sire:

The sun is as warm on my skin as ever, but today
the light seems more slanting, with a weakness that
finally allows colors to show themselves, and I feel
restless, as if preparing for a voyage. Receiving from
Your Excellency these past days the request to polish
up Don Quixote's rusty armour, buckle on his spurs, and
send him on his way to the Middle Kingdom, there to
serve Your Excellency, confident in the good reception
and honor with which Your Excellency favors books
of all sorts, but especially those that attack the vulgar

and dissolute tastes of these times, I must humbly beg, with all the obeisance that I owe such grandeur, Your Excellency's mercy and understanding in being unable to do more than lay before Your Excellency's eyes the true *Second Part of the Ingenious Caballero Don Quixote de la Mancha,* in which is recounted the death of the Dolorous Knight. For, alas, it is true that Don Quixote has been put into the sack. He is now truly dead.

I say "the true *Second Part*" because a year ago, a weasel, supposedly from Tordesilla, who calls himself Alonso Fernando de Avellaneda, published a false *Second Part.* I was just then translating a newly discovered packet of papers by Cide Hamete Benengeli that tells of the further adventures of Don Quixote after he recovers from his madness. Imagine my chagrin. But, though the weasel has been in my chicken coop and steals my money and my fame, he has not stolen Don Quixote. By parading around a disgusting, scurrilous, and gross facsimile, he is like that madman I once saw in the streets of Seville who inflated dogs with a straw through the anus. Calumny, with her long ass's ears, has been twirling through the streets like autumn chestnut leaves. I must now defend myself, but it is not so easy for a storyteller to claim to be a truth-sayer.

In this profession, I have learned a thing or two, and have enjoyed myself doing so: *dulce et utile,* said Horace, make good poetry. I have learned that we all speak the language of others, though that language is a vast terrain of unavoidable carelessnesses, full of sink-holes, chasms, mirage-like lakes, dangerous quicksands. Everything and anything can be said and denied at the same time, including that truth-saying is possible. Adam spoke the language of truth, but all we others speak a fallen language. The poet doesn't invent his words; they come to him readymade, and all our utterances resonate with the din of everyone else's speech. I am like the house-builder, who gathers up the mud and stones and wood he finds around him and forms them into something that serves. We may not actually create anything, since the mud and stones and words were already there, but we build something, which is all the word *poet* means, a maker. And it doesn't matter to us whether the stones were used before, or if indeed they really are stones, as long as our houses protect us from the battering rain, warms us, gives us solace and a home.

If words are stones and houses are stories, words are still not stones, nor are stories houses, even if we can dwell in stories, though not as we dwell in houses. Your Majesty hears how we talk, so distant from speaking the truth. I have learned that whatever I say, the listener will think what he wants to think. If I say that I don't want to tell him the name of Quixote's village, he still looks for it, then tells me it is Argamasilla in La Mancha. If I say that Quixote's name is Quexana or Quijada or Quesada, or that it doesn't matter what it is, he still thinks it is Quixote and argues about it. And if I say that I don't deviate one iota from the truth, he thinks I am lying. What will he think if I tell him that I lie? That I lie by saying that I lie, so I tell the truth, or that I tell the truth, and am therefore lying? A cheap trick of logic, one might object, but the trick, I answer, is in the speaking.

I am told that in Your Highness's land, men speak in pictures (though I saw no pictures in the letter delivered to me). I think pictures lie as much as words. It is true that if I say I lost my arm at the Battle of Lepanto, Your Majesty would still not know if I write with my right or left hand, while if I sent my portrait, Your Majesty would know instantly. Yet I have never seen a peasant try to yoke a picture of oxen. Only a madman would do that, madmen and historians, who think language tells the truth. But with words, we are always saying one thing for another, for words are only figures of other words. If I tell Your Highness about the beauties of the ancient Cathedral of Salamanca, I call that church a *cathedral* because it contains the bishop's *cathedra,* or chair, which is itself a figure for the bishop's see or *sede* or *seat,* and I call the building a church *(iglesia),* because *iglesia* comes from the Latin *ecclesia,* which is a figure for the Greek word *ekklesia,* meaning "congregating together." And *Salamanca,* which Polybius reports as Helmantica may be the name of an ancient god mispronounced, or Polybius's mistake of Salmantica, meaning a "place by a running stream."

So, though people might say that I am a liar, I do not know how that can be. Sometimes I wake in the night and am so worried that I can no longer sleep, and only in the morning do I realize that my worry was left over from the day before. Just this morning, in the early dimness, I clearly saw two mosquitoes hovering close to my face and, trying with one quick slap to catch them both at once, realized that I was in the bright light of day, the sun a white square on the wall against the bed. I do not think I lied to myself, yet cannot imagine how such a thing could be, unless I am not who I am.

Your Excellency, however, is who he is, he who gives universal umbrage to the arts, whose literary acumen surpasses all others in perfection, and thus who will understand me perfectly when I say that I send him the genuine, actual, verifiable ending of the story of our gentle knight, and Your Excellency will easily discern the true Don Quixote from Avellaneda's despicable imitation.

In the *Second Part* of our humble history, Cide Hamete Benengeli narrates the tragic manner of the demise of Don Quixote, who here must run a long race against Death, whose human face he sees among a group of masquers at the very beginning of these adventures, and who tracks him throughout the history in the guise of the bachelor Sansón Carrasco, the indefatigable and jocular instrument of the misbegotten and gone-awry plans of the priest and the barber to trick Don Quixote into staying peacefully at home for the rest of his days. From the moment the false Don Quixote, crude and ignorant a copy as he is, appeared in the fake sequel written by the reptilian Avellaneda, the end of the true Don Quixote was decreed, for his life, having sun-ripened slowly on the Hesperian tree of Cide Hamete's history, could only be protected from Avellaneda's worms by the plucking: and so the *Second Part* is like a long parenthesis, a hiatus lengthened by pleasurable inventions, adventures, and discussions, but whose closure must always be expected, casting a moonlight hue on all the knight's energies. Your Excellency will see that the wit and invention and ingenuity that, in the *First Part,* are Don Quixote's lifeblood, filling him with a life of thoughts, passions, experiences, anger and tenderness, desires and obligations, percepts and concepts, are, in the *Second Part,* the preservatives of his body, such that Your Excellency now holds in his hands the bound and decorated mummy of what once was a man.

Yet I cannot wish it any other way. Ten years ago, when I finished the *First Part,* I was content to let Don Quixote wander unattended through the realm, becoming a folk hero, appearing in tattered armour at local festivals, hooted at by barefoot boys, barked at by ribby dogs, pebbles bouncing off his dusty helm. Perhaps I thought of him then as being in another kind of sack, the puppet sack of the mysterious Ginés de Pasamonte, the one he carried with him when he put a green taffeta patch over his left eye and became Maese Pedro, the puppeteer who traveled Eastern La Mancha with a talking ape. Like words, the Don could be taken out and deployed in ever new stories. Only upon reading Avellaneda's feigned sequel did I realize that I, who had given him life, had also made him vulnerable, had abandoned him to become, helplessly, something he was not: a crude figure of medieval farce; that I and only I—who had somehow allowed him, as no other figure before in literature, to grow into personhood, provoking the sympathy and concern of everyday readers—could rescue him once again from being a stock figure by the simple exertion of superior wit and invention and ingenuity, for the only difference between my truth and Avellaneda's falsehood lies in my superiority to him as a writer, shallow, shallow, shallow; that everything he invented in his sequel I could surpass; and that in thus surpassing him, I could restore Don Quixote to manhood and, with him, Sancho Panza. The Tordesillescan may play with the joke that the magician Alquife writes the feigned story of Don Quixote, but the real Don Quixote and Sancho Panza can deliberate on the truth of Cide Hamete's history, can consider the differences between history and poetry in the telling of truth, can correct both authorial mistakes and printer's errors from the published version of the *First Part*, can wonder with surprise and terror at how the author can know all their intimate adventures, especially since they thought they were alone at the time, can criticize the writing and the storytelling, can meditate on their author's motivations, can project future fictions as possible heroic material for further histories (all of which will be true, as only they and I know the truth of their authorship)—can, furthermore, discuss and demonstrate the ignorance, lies, and fallacies of the Tordesillescan and his false *Second Part.* They can meet other characters who have read the *First Part* and even the *Second Part* as it unrolls, and thus can watch Don Quixote and Sancho Panza as if they were characters in a novel, which they are, watch them aesthetically and from some psychic distance, even manipulating them as if they were characters of their own, with whom Don Quixote and Sancho then discourse, showing themselves thus to be vastly superior in wit to the dull and imitative Avellaneda. And through such discourse, they can approach the lofty subject of how they can be living people with their own free will and yet, moment by moment, someone else's characters, a grappling that exposes their and our condition in life.

If sluggish Avellaneda shows the reader an arrogant and insane Don Quixote as he disputes a pragmatic, realistic, and cheating Sancho in a boring is-so-isn't-so argument about whether an inn is a castle or not, I show Don Quixote and Sancho seeing the same moon-faced, snub-nosed country girl and her friends but arguing their differing uses of that reality, implicating in their shifting argument both deceptions and self-deceptions, as well as their changing needs, their diverging roles, the rhetoric they have learned from each other and the ironies of their history together, with Don Quixote insisting that the three peasant girls are what they are while Sancho creates from them the princess Dulcinea and her two handmaidens, both arguing such convolutions of intent that they play upon each other's wits like taws upon a schoolboy's bottom until Don Quixote, bolstered by the actuality of what he sees, believes that Dulcinea, whom he'd previously known to be his own invention, is truly real, though imperceptible to his eyes, while Sancho, caught up in the language of poetry, must deal with truthful lies and lying truths, as if he were the Great Commentator Averroes explicating Plato's cave of falsehood. If the false Quixote, like the Devil's companion Suero, beats up all the people who want to cross his bridge and thinks only of fighting, mine discourses on all the subjects of humanism—poetry, justice, government, history, arms, friendship—and so, too, does Sancho, as indeed all good men, honest men, pious men should. In truth I could not have thought of a better ploy to further Don Quixote's fame than the publication of a false *Second Part*, and had the Tordesillescan not written it, I would have had to, for everything he's done has been turned to account. I have stolen his every feeble idea to make Don Quixote ever more lifelike, ever a new kind of being whom the world has never before seen, a living, breathing, thinking, feeling person with whom everyone can sympathize, converse, banter, argue, who can be mocked, befriended, judged, hurt, loved, belittled, admired, feared, and angered, who gives and receives consideration and advice and wisdom and folly, whose turns of mood and wit and mind are always surprising and yet in character, and to whom we are attached in our own imaginations, so that, as if having another human being within ourselves, we grow by enlargening our knowledge of him, yet who is only made of words.

To simple Avellaneda, then, I owe the simple truth of the mirror and its doubling, illusory reflection, which nevertheless shadows forth a truthful image, his dull reflection of me showing me who I truly am, and so I build a world of mirrors around Don Quixote, a theater of reflections to make his wit double back on itself, Chinese boxes of shadows. Sancho becomes Don Quixote, plays the role of Don Quixote to his wife's Sancho, much as he, later, with the three country lasses, plays the role of Don Quixote to Don Quixote himself. They meet the masquers, whose allegorical representation of life reflects Don Quixote's being, and though he recognizes the familiarity of this allegorical world, he is not yet able to see that he himself, dressed like a masquer in the costume of a knight, fulfills the role of the knight errant that he himself has noticed is missing from the company of players. And in his encounter with the Knight of the Woods, Don Quixote not only meets another insane knight errant, but discovers that this knight, who is none other than the scholar Carrasco in disguise, has met the false Don Quixote, while Don Quixote himself hides his own identity by pretending to be his own best friend, and when the sun dawns upon this scene of bewildering shadows, disguises, and reflected identities, the Knight of the Woods reveals himself to be the Knight of the Mirrors, whose armour is covered by countless mirrors in the shape of moons, itself a lunatic reflection. And, many adventures later, at the novel's end, it is of course Carrasco, again transformed, this time into the Knight of the Blank Moon, who defeats Don Quixote in combat, though without ever touching him, and who thus forces his retirement, this mirage-like battle between Don Quixote and his own image bringing on sanity and death.

Even Cide Hamete Benengeli—and can a man, even an Arab, be named Eggplant—finds himself reflected in these mirrors, for, following Don Quixote's theatrical apothegm that actors and plays mirror all of human life, because while the play is on, the actors all dress according to their roles, but after the play is over, they put off their costumes and all become equal, the historian needs to, and does, describe in detail, as if preparing for the great unrobing, the clothing and costumes of all his personages, beginning from the first page with the green wool vest and Toledo red cap that Don Quixote wears in bed: the ten-layer-thick embroidery that Dulcinea wears; the Knight of the Mirrors' overvest of fine gold; Don Diego de Miranda's green overcoat edged in tawny velvet and his tawny velvet cap; Don Quixote's Walloon breeches, chamois vest, soft, open-necked blouse, waxed shoes, and dark brown cape, which he wears indoors; and the black robe covered with flames and the conical hat with images of devils that Sancho has to wear at the funeral of Altisidora. It's as if, for Cide Hamete, clothes have become the woven *contextus* of fate, like the taffeta, linen, satin, and velvet cloths that my sister Andrea received from Locadelo as a judgment for her paternity suit and which she later pawned to ransom me from Algiers, or like a warp of green against a woof of pink, which can make a cloth light up with iridescence, imitating the dark flashings of bird wings, or like the constant weaving of wit, of antithetical words, vocabularies, metaphors, and puns that undertwine and overlay each other in an endless fabric of storytelling.

If the world around Don Quixote mirrors him, then his life in the *Second Part* is continually self-revealing, every encounter like two stags with locked horns. Have I mentioned that my family name is Spanish for stag? In Algeria, people called me Ben al-Ajejil, which my *morisco* translator tells me means son of a stag, so Cide Hamete Benengeli and I share the same name, because *Benengeli* is only a printer's error for *Benenjejeli*. Echo is the disembodied voice of reflection, and, as Tiresias the blind—who, because he saw himself as someone else, was both man and woman—predicted of Narcissus, who always saw himself only as himself, death is the outcome of knowing oneself. Know that you are mortal, said the ancients. This, too, I owe the Tordesillescan.

But enough of the Tordesillescan. I've become a garrulous old man, and he is only the scuffling thrum in my ears. I gathered a language, Your Excellency, which he could never touch, a playful and witty speech of sayings, proverbs, and adages, in which I could speak of the highest subjects next to the lowest, in which the greatest fantasies sound natural and everyday, heaven brought to earth and the commonplace raised, in which insanity sounds sane and the normal, mad, and this is the wagging of tongues that brought Don Quixote to life.

Don Quixote has died, and only by his dying am I now able to conceive him as having lived. He was first Don Quexana, and although so much has passed in these many years that I cannot even count them, I see him with great clarity because only yesterday, my *morisco* translator, Abd al Aziz al Rahman Badawi, brought me his discovery of Cide Hamete's account of his first meeting with Don Quixote, and in the clear light of that past, I seem to see myself, too. When Cide Hamete first encountered Don Quexana, he was riding out of the courtyard of the inn in the village of Argamasilla. In those days, said Abd al-Aziz, Cide Hamete had a pet mosquito who came to him when called and who accompanied him everywhere on walks. That day, his mosquito said, "Look over there, Hamete. See that haughty Cide over there, so thin I could not get any food from him. You need to write a story about how thin he is. What is holding him up, anyway? If he were to wear a suit of armor, no matter how old it might be, it would hold him up straight like that, but when he took it off, he would be left crumpled like a shepherd's hook. That's the thing about armour, you know. It all looks alike, so when two knights ride at each other in a tournament, it's like two stags going at each other. You can't tell who is who. Go talk to him and find out what makes him strut about so upright and straight."

You may say, "There goes Miguel again, lying about Cide Hamete's pet mosquito. How can a mosquito talk?" But I answer you that I am telling the truth. My *morisco* translator Abd al-Azis al Rahman Badawi is a mosquito.

As Cide Hamete writes, his only thought on glancing at the old man his mosquito had pointed out was the farce of his regal bearing: the haughtiness of his stride, his long, straight back, the oratorical gestures of his hands, his lifted face, the distant look in his eyes, which peered over the heads of his interlocutors and which, coupled with the poverty of his dress and the emaciated form of his body, his disheveled grey hair, hollow cheeks, and sallow complexion, spoke of the dark hallways and dusty pantries of our country gentlemen. Cide Hamete observed him for some time in the weak morning sunlight, perhaps it was a day like today, halting his dapple at the entrance of the courtyard to allow the man and several others in leisurely conversation with him to pass, and this first impression of the incongruity between the man's reality and who he seemed to think he was became fixed in Hamete's mind for weeks until, having had to return to La Mancha, he saw Don Quejana several more times at the inn, engaged in heated conversations with his village companions. One evening by the fire, when the man and his friends were discussing the adventure of Florestan and Galaor at the fountain of Olmos—how Florestan, having thrice defeated the villains with his long and probing lance, appeared enormously attractive to all three of the beautiful damsels he'd just saved, and how he could have bedded them all, but instead chose to return the first to her lover, to take only the second, and to give the third to his brother Galaor, whom he so extolled as an equally well-endowed and powerful knight, and handsome as well, that the hesitant maiden was persuaded to give herself to his brother in full delight—in the midst of such discussions, Cide Hamete interrupted to ask if he did not find it unseemly that an old man such as himself, surely well past fifty, as was the Cide, could take such titillating pleasure in the sexual exploits of these figures, arguing with other old men about the number of times handsome Galaor slept with lovely women or lecherously wondering if the princess-to-be-queen Briolanja had slept with Amadis before marrying his brother Galaor.

Don Quexana looked at me a long time in the dim fire-light after I'd finished, writes Cide Hamete Benengeli, and seemed to see me with difficulty. Perhaps he was short of sight or had old eyes or was somewhat blind. Finally, finding my dim form across the room, he repri-manded me for my lack of courtesy in intruding into a conversation among friends, though he acknowl-edged the apparent criticism of my question, going on to say that while it was true that in romances, all good knights were young, well-formed, athletic, powerful, and well-mannered, and all girls were likewise young, beautifully proportioned, and full bosomed, with tight stomachs and comely thighs, these commonplaces of courtly romances embody the radical moral philosophy of *courtoisie*. Just as a person's courtesy demonstrates the inner virtue of gentility, so a person's outer, physical form reveals inner sexual prowess. Thus, in this ideal world, every young maid may identify the right kind of man with whom to spend the night. All romances focus on dalliance, sexual play, flirtation, and conquest, and the other theme of romance, namely fighting, is merely the means by which sexual pleasures can be achieved, acting both to exhibit sexual energy in another form and to attract the properly matched partner for the bed. All this might seem frivolous to me, Don Quexana lectured, but romances serve a civic and humanitarian function by allowing those who are not handsome or sexually attractive—who do not move with gracious distinction, who are, like myself and like him, old and ugly, like most if not all the people of the world—to participate vicariously in fantasies of desire. Because the pleasures of the text are erotic ones, they allow us all to be stronger, braver, and more vigorous than we are, they endow us with loveliness and attractiveness and the pleasures that reward such beauty, and they surround us with a world of plenty, of the possibility of plenty, where all that is needed or desired is available, even those things that may be illicit or shameful.

I, writes Cide Hamete, was so surprised by this answer that I remained silent as he continued.

Such has always been the nature of poetry. In the damp days of creation, men would stamp their feet to the flicker of firelight, singing and enacting the grief and joy of circumstances, both sudden and unexpected, which brought success or failure to longings, even those that were unspoken mysteries of ignorance and incomprehension. They danced and prayed and gave shuddering offerings from scant supplies, until—as in hunt one person always makes a first movement—one man cried out in a lone voice to speak and dance and pray for all the others, and when he did, the others fell silent in order to watch and listen, their voices now speaking inside themselves, in unison with the one man, and at that parturient moment, the hero was born, the leader, the scapegoat, the man who is like us but better than we, who symbolizes us but is responsible for us, this reflection of our desires from which we hide. And in that separation from that one voice, we became the flock, the chorus, the congregation, the community, saving ourselves from his certain catastrophe. Poetry was born as metaphor, religion was born as surrogate, the polis was born as emulation, consciousness was born as inner speech. And so, he concluded his diatribe, we old and ugly men are the participating tribal community for chivalric and pastoral romances, the donkey's tail of an ancient tradition, filling the interstices of these fabulous adventures with our would-be wet dreams.

Your Excellency, in my mind I can see that moment so clearly, I see myself so clearly that I cannot say all that I thought or perceived. I heard in Don Quexana's ingenious reasoning to justify his common and prurient appetite the cheerful voice of my demented mother saying to me one morning upon rising that she'd realized in the night that she had no reason to be depressed over the infection in her left pupil because she finally remembered that years ago she had exchanged her left eye for a glass one, and everyone knows that glass cannot be infected. Yet, though I heard my mother, God rest her soul, inflected in Don Quexana's rhetoric, hearing her did not sadden me as before but enthralled me instead, made me want to laugh out loud, which I did when the *morisco* was reading me Cide Hamete's manuscript. Cide Hamete himself, in his story, began to chortle and harrumph and garruff to himself under the frowning stares of Don Quexana and his friends. He recognized immediately that Don Quexana's ability to defend his craziness with wit and reason, at once righting his lunacy and leavening his madness, made him a fitter subject for wit and farce than the fanciful peasant Bartolo, who merely thought he was a knight errant. And even as Cide Hamete sat in the shadows of the dying fire, listening with half an ear to the old men and their choral appreciations of famous lovers— of Launcelot and Queen Guinevere, of Pyramus and Thisbe, of Basilio and Quiteria the beautiful—his mind filled with imaginings of gleeful incidents that further tested his decorous self-restraint, and he was forced to retire early to bed to entertain his new project of writing the narrative of Don Quexana.

Though Quexana became Quixote that evening in Argamasilla, he was not yet the Quixote we know, for when I contracted with Juan de la Cuesta to undertake the retelling of Cide Hamete's history, I was not entirely free of Bartolo, so Don Quixote began his adventures as if he were only a peasant whose mind had been addled by too much reading, as if he had been hit on the head by a stone occasioning some small mechanical defect in the brain, and so he had a difficult start, the unsympathetic world battering him harshly as he struck one pose after another like a patient in an asylum, until, desperate to keep the story going, to fulfill Cuesta's contract, I listened to the advice of the innkeeper, the first friendly person Don Quixote encountered, who explained that Don Quixote needed to return home to get himself some money, some shirts, and a page. So it was that the fat innkeeper who was transformed into Sancho Panza made all the difference in the world—that and the need to keep the story going, an endless tale, like the one Sancho tells of the shepherd who ferries his goats across the Guadiana River, first one, then another, then the next, then another, then another, a story that ends and only ends when the listener forgets to follow it. I continued and Don Quixote continued, and with each new device to further his life, interpolating stories within stories with recurring characters and newly discovered manuscripts, I discovered more about Don Quixote. Quexana's haughty bearing and twisting fantasy were aspects of a character for whom chivalry, romantic identification, and love of wisdom and knowledge were also consonant, so that his dementia, because it was totally functional and reasonable, was no more than fantasy and reason and care operating in the daily world—was, thus, a critique of sanity itself, a revelation of the place of fantasy within reason; or so it became under the guise of Don Quixote.

Never before had a figure in poetry been so free of its creator or of its readers. Ancient poets fixed a morality on their heroes, and, as moral character encountered storied circumstances, the heroes' ethical choices revealed that character and also determined the future of their lives. But Quixote, being mad, is free to act apart from his moral center and from the circumstances he finds himself in, and I, who am his creator, am free to invent any action, though to explain that action I must repeatedly put myself in his wit and speak out of his mania, as if he were someone else, and so he is, so that he is less my spokesman than I am his. He has escaped authority, and he gives me free reign of invention. How ironic that Quexana, who espoused the hero as a communal, social figure of emulation and participation, should himself become in my book a surrogate for no one—not for the reader nor for the author, for who would identify with this crazy, old man—should become the new man, an individual severed from tribe and land, a figure who finds his own sufficiency in his own wit, invention, and ingenuity, not in mine, a single-point vanishing perspective that projects the individuation of himself into the dimensional organization of external space, so that he sees the world in perspective, sees it with consideration and forbearance and goodly patience. Because he is unpredictable, the imagination cannot emulate him but must stand apart, must judge him, consider him, respect him, love him as another person, as someone different from ourselves, and in so doing, our imaginations draw out our own individuality, creates our own self, validates our being. If we project ourselves onto the ancient hero, as Quexana said, in order to internalize his speech, speaking in his one voice for two parts of ourselves, and if, between ourselves and the hero, who is our projected selves, we make an inner space for consciousness, then with Quixote, we free our inner speech from this dependency, so that he is other to us as we are other to him. If Dante must delve into the deep structure of God's creation in order to understand—and by understanding to acquiesce to—God's love, thereby achieving humanity, his personhood measured by his conformity to a prior truth outside himself, then Don Quixote finds his humanity not in the preexistent conditions of the world, but rather in the free workings of his own imagination, free because of his madness: his percepts, precepts, and concepts creating his own external world and his own inner self.

I pause, Your Excellency, I pause to watch the motes drift in the sunlight outside my window and the small play of insects above the grasses, I pause because my pride holds onto this thing I have done in creating Don Quixote as a new man, I pause because I hear the sounds of myriad feet echoing to me out of the future, thousands and thousands and thousands of yet unborn people eager, pushing, hurrying to get to this now, this here, pressing on me a roar and a rumble I cannot ignore, as if I alone were the gatekeeper for their being, and not just for their physical existence but for their imaginative being, for the extent to which the everyday events of their lives will feel to them powerful or significant or consonant with their imagined stability of existence. They push me continually to validate their individuality—their self-sufficiency, their independence, their freedom—by creating for them, by describing textually for them, by securing for them a reality that scatters into the burrows of private experience an utterly shattered world. But I know better. I know that poetry is a ritual—religious, civic, and communal—that coming deeply from the poet's breath, it carries out into the world the airs that belong to his depths, that these come from his *manes*, his family, his commune, his tribe, his people as a congregation, because he is first and last formed in them, that as this breath arises voiced, vocalized in the language of his people, intoned, his tones will be peaceful and gay as the age is harmonious and balanced, strident and raucous as the age is chaotic, angry and resentful as the people suffer, and sorrowfully despondent when the people are lost. I know that the airs of poetry bond me to Castile, and they bond Castile to Castile. I know that poetry speaks of and to the ritualizing and regularizing of the relations between man and woman, between lovers, between parent and child, between friends, among associates and acquaintances, between enemies. I know that poetry enriches human understanding and emotions, governs our perceptions of gains and losses, Heaven and Earth, rich and poor, the powerful and the governed, and so I know that all the forms of poetry— the epic and the pastoral, the comic and the tragic, the ode, the epithalamion, the sestina, the rondel, the ballade, the madrigal, the villanelle, the sonnet, the canzone—are rhythmed tonalities of civic rituals, that they teach the people and are like a good government. The ancient poet feels those rhythms beating in his heartblood and regulating the sounds his breath makes, and he feels certain that the stories he tells—the movements of the figures within those stories, the spread of the landscape, the speeches and thoughts of his characters, the pacing of events—all participate in these rhythms and airs. I have wanted to be a civic poet, a poet of the polis and the blood, to feel the tribal words flow through me and into me, yet I hear instead the clamour of thousands of unborn, future readers who do not want to listen to such airs. They want characters who see only from a single point of view, so that each is an image of himself and no other. They want a landscape that wraps around them, showing an individual perspective, one they are familiar with. They want stories and relationships and thoughts that are limited and detached like their own, so that their freedom will seem natural to them. They want to see themselves as other than, and they want me to portray for them a world in which that otherness flourishes. I hear them coming, and, tied as I am to Quixote's mania and his freedom, I hear their voices in me, so my poetry has always been a determined struggle, no phoenix I but an embarrassment, a jealousy, a rancour. Someday people will not struggle to write badly, for they will only write for themselves, and those who cannot write at all, who have no language, no community, no self, will nevertheless write poetry, write it freely and easily, and they will be my mad children.

Perhaps my ancestry is not pure, the tribal blood tainted, for some have said that Quixote is the bookeater Ezekiel, who prophesied the renewal during the Babylonian exile; that my caballero is a kabbalero; that Dulcinea is Schekhina, the female principle; that Quixote goes through the fourfold creation of Emanation, Formation, Creation, and Fabrication, as told in the *Sepher ha Zohar* of Moses Schem Tob de Leon of Avila, who is secretly referred to in the lion episode by the mention of Manuel Ponce de Leon, because Manuel is Hebrew for God's Glory, because Manuel and Moses both begin with the *M*, because *ponce* is a bridge, so forming a bridge between Don Quixote and Moses; that the four names of Don Quixote, namely

Quejana, Quexada, Quixote, and Quijano, are allegories of the four names of God, Elohim, Jehovah, Sebaoth, and Shadei; and that the apparent typographical error of Quixano is an anagram for *anochi*, the name in the *Zohar* that contains all sacred names: and, indeed, I have begun to hear the word *quijote* used to refer to the best cut of pork, as if it were a refinement of *marrano*, though the good Don eats no pork in the book. Whence this Jewish blood, I do not know, but something keeps the ancient words from coming, as if they fall through a thin crack in my head, while the usual words, the coarser stuff of everyday, rattle quick and sliding to mind.

Grandmother Leonora said her great-grandfather Juan Sánchez de Torreblanca was the first to set foot in the Indies, said she herself had seen Columbus, hair all white, sunlight and firelight playing round him as if an aureole, when he courted dark Beatrice in Cordoba, said she had seen him in the Torreblanca home make an egg stand on end, said Beatrice's son Ferdinand was sensitive and well-mannered but weak, said she thought all this was so, though it may have been before she was born, said the jar of slaked lime was cream and had to be restrained from drinking it all, my father picking her up from behind with her arms pinned, her feet kicking air, thick, white rivulets running out her laughing mouth which was screaming, *Help me, help me, rape, murder.* At the funeral, I was angry that people said she had died of folly. I was ten, and she had always been that way, just old beyond my boyish understanding. Yet something else besides my youth kept me from seeing her mania, for when my mother, too, lost herself, I still could not see it. I have not the easy clarity of sight that old poets have; I forever return to doubt and darkness.

She knew, better than I, when she began to lose her memory, hesitating on names, making up pet names to hide her forgetfulness, then angrily asserting, "You know who I mean, the man who is always at the corner," and though it seemed to us so gradual and imperceptible, her dark night cut her as suddenly as death, no crumbling of memory but a sudden blackness. She complained to Magdalena, but we only suggested that she write things down, leave notes for herself around the house, that forgetting was normal at her age, or perhaps the shock of my father's death had been too much, but she knew better, so that her lips became a firm, fixed line, and her eyes darted fear. One day we found her standing quietly on the next street, the despair gone. She had been looking for the house and cheerfully explained how she thought the house must have moved while she was at the market. She had reached that freedom in which Don Quixote lives, where, unconstrained by the authority of memory, her imagination constructed her everyday life. When neighbors brought her back from her wanderings, she was angry that total strangers had talked to her and treated her familiarly, had even known her family's intimate secrets, though she was sure they were pretending. She took Catalina to be my servant, and she never understood who Bela was. When she missed Rodrigo, she thought he had been kidnapped. For days and nights, she bemoaned his misfortune and carried in her small hands the old, yellowed copies of petitions she had submitted to the crown almost twenty years before when asking for my ransom from Algiers. How and where she had hidden them and found them again when she could remember nothing, I do not know. She worried them and read and re-read them, pacing the apartment, and when I explained that Rodrigo had died in the wars of Flanders, that the papers she read were for my ransom many years before, that I was the one who'd been a captive, she showed me that the appended documents of service were for Rodrigo, and it became too difficult to explain her own deceit to her, and, who knows, perhaps even then she had had confusions. Sometimes I would find her sitting by the window peacefully reading a scrap of writing from my table, but my relief was a delusion, for I realized that she could sit all day reading the same sentence over and over again, forgetting what she had read as soon as she read it and so never finishing a sentence with understanding. Or she sat on her small stool by the window surrounded by an enormous mat of tangled thread that grew larger as her swollen, arthritic fingers pecked at the tiny, incessant loops, enlargening some, tightening others, pulling over and under and through. She fumbled but worked steadily and without pause in the dim light. Time no longer held her cupped in his hands. She stayed up later and later, going to bed when the lightening sky surprised her and rising in the dark, so that the black of sleep ran into her dark waking without interruption, and her mind never woke to light of day. The needs of her body, too, fell away. She knew no hunger or forgot it soon after she knew it: ate voraciously when food was put before her; lost her appetite when it was taken away. Her bowels and bladder functioned without her or as we insisted. And though her black widow's dress of thin wool became tattered and bare and dirty because she would wear no other, yet she delighted in dressing slowly, humming to herself and smoothing down its sides and front caressingly as if preening.

With her sight dimmed, her hearing difficult, her memory scattered to the waters of Lethe, she was left to her inner self, her fears, her desires, her natural intellect and shrewdness, her imagination—those parts of ourselves that philosophers today call "characteristics"—so that while she lost herself, she also became more purely herself. When I told her that her school friends Margarita and Susana were dead, so the three of them could not have traipsed hand in hand in San Francisco the day before wearing provocatively low-cut dresses and followed by a handsome but slightly sinister gentleman in a green worsted suit with a green wool cape edged in tawny yellow, that it must have been a dream, she rebutted, "What can I believe if I do not believe in the things that my mind tells me." She was right, for what else was there but dandruff, the oily smell of dirty scalp, glistening skin seen through sparse white hair, the curling strands everywhere. Nothing could be truer or more sane, and her belief in the motions of her own mind, bolder than mine could ever be, constructed a more solid happiness than the sane could ever hope to experience. In Seville, there lived a madman who, when he sat before an empty stage, saw the most complicated and engaging stories acted out in front of his eyes by gifted and marvelous actors, but who was perfectly normal in every other part of life: who carried out his daily business with rectitude, was a helpful neighbor, responsible citizen, and an amiable host; and who lived his family life with love and affection. He was finally cured of his madness with hellebore and thereafter bemoaned that they had taken away the most delectable part of his life. In Seville was yet another man who thought all the ships that came into the river were his, and who was happy to be so wealthy. So, too, my mother's faith in her mind triumphed over her dysthemia, and so she was a little girl: she and Isabela chanted tongue-twisters together or told each other old tales of knights and lovers; while my sense of aporia remained many years after her death, remained, in fact, until, meeting with Quexana, I began to hear her voice in all of life.

Do we not all make mistakes, Your Excellency? I forget my glasses and look for them under the papers on my table, though they are in my pocket, where Catalina finds them. Lost in unrecoverable thought, I walk suddenly into posts, bump into swearing passers-by, fall sharply into holes in streets. When traveling in Andalusia, I was for many days rocked from morning till night on the back of a dappled ass, not knowing what I saw or heard, aware only that I had mounted in the morning and descended in the evening, not remembering if the day had been overcast or if the sun had shone, if I had passed through fields or through woods, nor whom I had seen or conversed with, what they had said or what I had answered. And often, especially now, in my old age, I read to the bottom of a page and do not understand a single thought, though I know I have read every word. Our lives seep through the rents in our consciousness while we pretend the cloth is whole. Every mistake is a small bit of insanity in my everyday life, which I hide by admitting my mistake. And what if we do not admit mistakes, as in all those disputes I have heard where each side holds firmly to its own blindness? The Duke tells Sancho that a good governor must hunt because hunting is the image of war and a test of leadership, that it is strength and intellect, and that is why aristocrats hunt and govern, but Sancho argues that hunting takes precious time from governing and may harm leadership by promoting killing without reason, that hunting and leisure should be the occupation of householders rather than of governors in a well-governed society. Neither can admit the other's fancy without denying his own, and so are not an aristocratic governor and a peasant both equally mad? And is Don Quixote attacking the puppets of Master Pedro because he truly believes them to be real a greater folly than the Duke and Duchess arranging elaborate hoaxes because they believe Don Quixote's madness to be real? And when I stayed with my mother despite knowing her to be completely demented, when I did her bidding, fulfilled her wishes, led her on with her fancies, talked to her reasonably, encouraged her, played the roles she gave me, was I not as insane as she? I repaid her in kind, Sancho Panza to her Don Quixote, accepting her folly for mine because she was who she was to me and I to her, because she cared for me and fed me my childish fantasies. We all do what our minds tell us to do and nothing more, and often, because of what the world says, much less. The comedy of Don Quixote is that he is more reasonable than he appears, and his tragedy is that he is defeated not by a more reasonable vision but by a less reasonable one.

And so, Your Excellency, I have become a different kind of writer from the ancient, fluent poet that I wanted to be, have become instead a poet of the prose of fancy and madness, a *vates* and a prophet, speaking as an outcast for the outcast, speaking without community in a language of the ordinary: a poet of the scholar in Salamanca who, through a strangely concocted love potion, was struck with phrenitis and, when revived, believed himself to be made of glass, the embrace of which state (that of his mortal fragility) allowed him to declare the truth of things fearlessly; a poet also of that reformed rake from Extremadura, who, because of his conversion, had grown rich, old, and paranoid, and whose extreme jealousy caused him to build for his beautiful, young wife in Seville a house modeled on her private parts, complete with a hayloft and watchman's dwelling, like a *mons venus*, above the main door, a tile-lined *vas vulvae* leading to an inner door, all the house's windows sealed up except to the sky; a poet, too, of that son of someone who, through reading too many books, set off to be a knight errant in the world and, for a brief span of time, was one, mirroring by his virtue, good works, charity, love, devotion, humility, simplicity, and generosity the world's use and abuse of power and control, its deceptions, injustices, and cruelties, and who thus, finally, shows us through fiction that balance between social reality and fantasy that exists in human polity.

I could go on, Your Excellency, I could tell you how the old poetic language was allied to the powers of autocracy, how the new, prosaic language I've invented is made up of the rhythms of democracy; I could give you more examples of everyday follies, such as the story of the parasite who lived in Valladolid when the court still resided in that city; I could distinguish for you the various kinds of mania—those based on an illness of judgment and those based on the distortion of perception—and the *loci* of these, whether in the humours or in the airy parts of the head or in the heavier parts of the bowels. I could tell you also of my new work, *Persiles and Sigismunda,* in which I follow the Biblical wisdom that we are all pilgrims on earth. But the slant of light is becoming rapidly more acute. The day grows still. I am the prattling court jester whom Your Excellency's grace has let in, fearful of Your Excellency's displeasure but driven to sing and prance in accordance with Your Excellency's beneficence. But now darkness and the lack of candles force me to discretion, and this humble servant begs leave to end.

CERVANTES'S 1616
LETTER TO THE EMPEROR

To Splendour, Sources, Red Earth, Sky, Breadth,
Ancestry, Great Potter, Emperor of the Ming,

Sire:

Though I was born in the dry and airy part of the year,
I drown in watery accumulation. The rains came late and
   heavy.
The cracked Manchegan soil soaked up the moisture
And, caking onto plowblades, ladened them.
The mired, dark oxen strain to turn the earth,
But the up-cast tillage packs tight,
And summer sun will bake it to rock. No seed
Will root through it, but I will be dead before disaster

Comes, drowned in my own hydropsical sea, pulled
Down tangled in long arms of watery drowse to cockled
Depths, dead when Your Majesty reads this letter. Water
Is everywhere, dripping from the clothes that steam before
The fire that Catalina burns all day, though wood
Is hard to find, puddling round her muddy clogs
By the door, rivuleting down the small windows,
Drumming on the roof and seeping through it,
Dangling threads that drill into the dirt floor, yet
With all this water in and out of me, I thirst,
Always wanting more.

I tell everyone I will die by Sunday,
But I am determined to set off for Madrid,
To finish my Prologue for *Persiles*, to keep
From dying in Esquivias. I have nothing against
This place, this twice rebuilt refuge of thirty years,
This house that I abandoned many times and
To which I returned each time, but the desolate, high plains
Of Mancha, windblown, endless, horizonless, thinned of air,
Place of hallucinations, mirages, spinning funnels
Of dust sucked up by listless summer skies, has never
Felt like home to me; even those people who've lived here for
Generations, like Catalina (for this was her father's house),
Grown hard, conservative from the sparsity of life,
Hold on for no love of place or spirit but for tenacity,
Without which lives here have no meaning at all.
And so they go on, children after parents,

Trying to be good, full of small sins, regulated
By the seasons, keeping customs but averting
Their eyes from the rest of the world. My stiff and
    thickened fingers
Are used to picking rotted, black parts off cabbage leaves,
My crusts of bread are as dry and hard as those of any
Manchegan peasant, I scrape the mold every
Week from dried sausages that hang darkly from
The roof, but I am no peasant to this country and will
Not die as one. Better to die in that white, clean room
In Madrid, with the noise of the world sounding through
The window, shoes set neatly beside the bed.

I don't regret Catalina. I have rooted in her
Deeply, past wet leaves and small pebbles, into her evenness
Of spirit, patience, hard work, her assumptions
Of faith and intimacy, with no twinge of meanness, no thought
Of vantage, and so our bond fulfilled the contract, continues
To do so, though Equivias is still no home. I had
No home when I met her, and thought I never would.
Ten years on foreign soils made Castile foreign to me.
Better to keep on moving, a prodigal sort of man.

We seemed then other people, so ignorant and young,
Though she was old for marriage and I into middle age,
So our bargaining was desperation, her father
Offering this farm and inheritance at his death
And I conflating the honor of my crippled arm

155

With the prospects of my plays, a citified and traveled
Dandy, ready to show his daughter at Court,
Friend and editor of Láinez, the only poet ever
To grace Esquivias. What hopes or disappointments
Our marriage roiled in her I do not know, but from
That tentative beginning she was true to me,
As if presaging, like a peasant, the time of harvest. She
And I would grow into something deeper and more
Human than love, and even that first year, when I brought
Isabela from Madrid, a light cloth over the basket
To shade her from the sun, she clucked to her, rocked her
In her arms, and silently prepared a place by our bed,
Knowing without asking that Bela was
My unspoken part of the contract.

                        I had little choice,
Though I do not think her mine, I had no money to settle
On her; her mother didn't want her, and had I left her,
She would have grown up, like Ana, servicing the men
At her father's inn. I make no excuses,
It was a long time ago.

                  Catalina brought
Her up, tended my dying mother, cared for me in
Those first years when I wrote *La Galatea*. She bartered
The grapes and olives and slaughtered the chickens, while I,
    like a madman,
Traveled Andalusia for the insatiable needs of the crown.

And when, as an old man, I settled in Valladolid to try
Once again at letters, she came from Esquivias,
A kerchiefed and solid countrywoman, to the bedecked fopperies
    of the Court,
And set up a second time our marriage bed, over
Which she wrote in green *Here Is No Dissension*, and she
Cared for me once more after fourteen years of absence
As I wrote *Don Quixote* and the *Exemplary Novellas*,
The fame of which discharged, finally, my part of her father's
    contract.

But that rooting was for life, not for death, so Esquivias
Remains her country, not mine, not one in which to plant my
    bones, nor—
To invoke the ancient Manchegan *genius loci*—to hallow
My plot with the sacred voice of crumbling headstones. Mancha
Is part of me, but I am not of La Mancha, and in
Her shaded cemeteries, where I step softly, pitted,
Streaked marbles call me passer-by. Perhaps
That is why I am no poet.

I left home before home, a first flight, and in Cabra
Churchyard, I heard the dead cry in the night, echoing
My sobs. The bats whorled overhead, the crickets screamed,
I pressed my nose to the base of a tomb and sniffed the evil
Odour of spiders in their lairs, snails dragging their trailing
Progress through the dust. The midnight shrieked of cocks,
The silence, cold, circled in footsteps, till I woke in midday heat.

I remember the fear without fearing, as all
My memories now seem without feeling, successive
Backdrops, lived one after the other by someone else
Already dead. In the rushes by the edge of a pond, I tried
To catch tadpoles to eat, but they slipped quicker than my grasp.
Some mill attendants gave me a handful of flour. I hid in
A ruined house, where the moon spoke through the broken roof.
A one-legged man showed me how to trap the fatty muskrat
By the stream's edge and for the first time split my buttocks. I ran.
I woke one morning under an oak tree hung with corpses,
Their loosened pants draping their ankles, thin and naked, their
Shit-streaked thighs, heads all cockeyed, empty eye sockets.
A traveling troupe of players took me in to feed
The oxen, carry water, set out the benches, hawk
The shows, polish the swords and helmets. Once I
Memorized lines and played the role of the ingenue.
And when darkness cut the days short and the players' breaths
Hung in the dim evening light and mist and hoarfrost
Pressed upon the land, I returned to my mother's house,
Just past my twelfth name day.

                      O, how young I was, though I
Seemed not to know it, my memory never sufficient
To what I really was, always seeing myself
As someone else and always from the present, as if
That twelve-year-old boy had the equanimity
Of a sixty-year-old man, so when I see today

A boy on the road, I stare and wonder disbelieving,
I never was so young. All our past is subject
To our present, forgetting some parts, remembering others,
Revising as we go, repeating the stories we
Have told with one emphasis and then with another, as befits
The listeners and the situations of the telling, though we seem
Unable to imagine beyond our present tale,
For all our present selves are the momentary story
Of our past. What we know, moment by moment, what
We experience as life, are nuances of the change
We cast upon our memories. A sudden illumination
Lights up what we once were. Every face seen clearly,
Every irony understood, alters irrevocably who
We remember having been. I never was twelve, never
Did those things. It's only a story I tell to keep
Alive, but when I die, the story stops, the clouds
Hold still, revisions will have to cease. The moment by moment
Flux of thoughts and feelings, sense, desire, will no longer
Work its prevarications, constructions, and accommodations
On my *me.* I will be twelve years old again,
As I really was, this old man's body falling
Away from him as he runs jostling through the crowd
By the Giralda to hold the gentleman's white horse
While he goes in the chapel to pray. I will be that
Boy of fourteen again, awakened from sleep on the road
To Salamanca by the liberal and gentle Juan Fortuny,
Taken to university as his servant, and, in accordance with
The custom at that school, allowed to follow my master's

Course of study and so, for four years, to perfect myself
Diligently in law and human letters. And Tomás,
Tomás, before he was fat and old and dead, when
He will again be witty, clever, interested in all things,
We will walk the fragrant, freshly cut stubble fields from Classe,
Where the fleet docks, to the round brick campanile
Of Sant'Apollinare, rising above the flats,
To view the mystery of the transfiguration depicted
In its catino, and alone in the soft even light of
The apse, our voices hollow, we will look up like two
Of twelve sinful lambs among the lilies, Tomás
Piecing together the mystical anagram, part in Greek,
Part in Latin, part in hieroglyphics, that says,
Jesus Christ, son of God, saviour, beginning and end
Of life, redeemer of the world.

                Change stops, there are no possibilities
Of past or future, no subjunctives of desire.
We talk, and I want to hear Bela in herself, as she
Understands herself, saying what she says
At that moment, while wanting her to hear me as I am
In myself, to hear herself as if she were
Not in herself as she speaks. I hope for, wish for, a small
Opening in Isabela, but when I die, that desire
Will end, too, for that desire is a desire for the possibility
Of my future, which will resound and harmonize
The present and the past, a desire for her living, for time,
For who she is face to face with me, there where she is,

Estranged. When I die, the present will disappear and reveal
All the past that it has always hidden. The past
And the future, which is only the desire to remake
The past, can then be fixed forever, as Quixote's
Death freed him from tampering fools, his endless story of time
Now fixed in words, and though subject to varying interpretations,
He will be, in the beginning as in the end, purely
A timeless text. My death, too, will make me a work
Of art, a novel, as if written, sanctified in
Its own way. What might have been will no longer differ
From what could or would be, every part of me
Transfigured into what truly was, the illusion
Of perspective folded into monumental
Frontality like a Byzantine mosaic. While in life
I am as insubstantial as a moment, in death,
I will be embraced as certainty.

                                       I go towards death as if
It were my first home now, returned from a long campaign,
From the cold of standing sentry, the danger of assaults, from fear
During battles, hunger of sieges, ruination of minefields,
The heavy charges of soldiering life, and from its lighter
But more wearing needs, too, the need to bully and steal and
    cheat,
To use the commissary or quartermaster's power,
To deal with tight-fisted, devious paymasters and be tight-fisted
    and devious
In turn, always requisitioning more than needed, quarreling

With billeted hosts, insolent new recruits, complaining
Townspeople, to see daily what is not right and have
To do it, too, but returned also with memories
Of a wilder, more liberal time—hot male camaraderie,
Red and blue houses bright in the light of the Neapolitan sun,
The wealth of Milan, Palermo's comfortable dwellings, Rome's
Broken marbles, Italian wines, gay uniforms—of suave
Treviano and brave Montefrascón, of Asperino's fabulous
Strength, the generosity of the Greeks Candía and Soma,
The sweet softness of Señora Garnacha, and, once arrived home,
Perhaps I will find what Your Excellency seeks,
Clean and direct speech, which in Christiandom
We teach as only what Adam and the angels speak. Till then
I speak this earthly tongue, at once opaque and revealing
And full of our convoluted weaknesses.

                                        The other day,
In Madrid, I saw a woman turn and suddenly hail a man
On the other side of the street. She wore a dark green velvet
Dress, broadly edged in black, and must have been past forty,
Though she held her back arched like a young woman. Her eyes
Were dark and glistened. "Ah," she said loudly, "Don't I
Know your name, and what is your name?" Her equally well-
Dressed companion, a woman younger than she,
Frowned at this sudden indiscretion. The man, taken aback
At first, as if she were a total stranger, as I
Believe she was, hurried across the street on seeing
How strikingly beautiful she was and introduced himself.

The woman, seeing him closer—the tattered red feathers in his
    cap,
The lace at his throat and wrists a bit mottled, hair and beard
Unkempt—became apathetic and carried on a disinterested
Conversation about the narrowness of the street,
But her young companion grew quickly attentive and witty.
She and the man, who now addressed his words to her,
Said clever little things and laughed, and when they parted, they
    hoped
To see each other on the Prado. Though I have prepared
For death, I still laugh to recall this *vanitas,*
For that is how speech in this world is spoken, full
Of clear intentions, but never saying what it says.

Still in thrall to the present, I'm in no hurry to go home.
My swollen body does all the work: these bloated legs
And joints, my wrist and fingers so large I can barely hold
This feather that scratches and blotches the page with hen tracks,
My writing illegible like my father's. This tangled, kenning
Language, its defects and transgressions, is the only one I know;
Mirroring our very lives, it holds us to the mysteries.
Who knows their origins, those imperfections of character
We were born to, which (hidden from our very selves)
Unroll the story of our lives, a story that, nonetheless,
May not, if ever, be true?

The windless rain is relentless, crashes onto the earth.
I am not dying, except that we all die from birth.

I hear the rain, I smell the body's exhalations,
I see the wavering shadows slide across this page. I'm
As alive as I've always been, though naturally weakened by age,
Not dying like my mother's long death, struck dumb, mouth
    gasping open
For air, blistered and bloody, unable to swallow water,
Fear in her eyes, a long, long dying, nor like the two men
I saw beaten to death among the Turks when I was captured,
The first I did not know, but the second, I've
Forgotten his name, came from Cataluña, a hardened
And reckless sailor, both whipped to death for failed escapes,
An hour at least of bloody scourgings that left their bodies
Congeries of meat and bones, quivering and trembling entirely
On their own, their throats finally cut to stop their pumping
Hearts, nor like Juana's quiet expiration in the old cottage
On Calle de Leon, around the corner from the Prince
Of Morocco's home, lulled to deep sleep late at night as
Constanza and I recited Láinez's old poems to her.

No, I am not yet in the throes of dying, only heavy
With dropsical pain, but knowing I will die soon, I cannot
Stop thinking of death and of life. Some clever person said
Death was a non-event, but so seems life to me,
Much having passed without my realizing, much
Of the rest forgotten, whether from weakness of mind or shame,
Even as I sift my past from others. I
Have tried to recall my capture and tell it
As hero or thief, but things are not so simple.

What will Algiers be like when my self drops off
Along with this body and it all comes flooding back
At once in the brilliant space of happening, every detail
Clearer than memory in its pure reality
Without my self to forestall it, when such complexity
As I cannot now fathom becomes as simple as truth
Should be? Like Scheherazade, I learned to tell stories
For my life there, I learned to story my life.
Algiers was and is a dream through which always sounds
The muezzin call to prayer, and other than that distant,
    mellifluous
Chant that falls to me from the sky, it is silence and light.
I lived for once, and for that once only, above my rank
And station, for what rank can prisoners have when facing
Slavery? How I escaped enslavement, the galleys, the quarries,
Or the fields, I do not know, whether because of my maimed
    hand or
The letter I carried from Don Juan or Dali's love of me,
It doesn't matter now. But then it gave me more
Than life, since in the *bagnios* with those awaiting ransom,
I lived freely with lords and gentlemen. We hadn't
Much food, our clothes were ragged, we wore irons, but during
    the day,
I wandered the city and soon added to our stores, so
That once, while waiting for Rodrigo's frigate, I fed fourteen
Of us for five months, hidden in a cave by the sea. I,
A mere soldier, actor, and *picaro*, was leader among men in Algiers,
For captivity, like leveling death, freed us from custom and law,

And we all became hero or coward, fool or wise man,
Lover or villain, cruel or kind, vengeful or sweet,
As we were or as we chose to be. I chose
To play the hero and played it convincingly, led three escapes,
Was sentenced to a thousand lashes, but was spared for Agi's sake.

Algiers was the truest city I have ever been,
Larger than any in Spain and older than even Rome,
Filled, like God's creation, with people of every type,
Though we call them all Turks: leather-capped Berber
    tribesmen
From the inner land, a white-clad black mkungu from beyond,
Hundreds of Egyptian shopkeepers
From Alexandria or Cairo, Moghrabian muleteers, Arabians
From the desert to the east, who kept hostelries for their Bedouin
Fellows, Persian poets, Tunisian dancers, Moghul
Musicians and singers, veiled and masked Muslim women,
Their eye-holes circled dots or hatched like prison bars,
Greek and Turkish soldiers of the Odjaq, Abyssinian
Artisans, perhaps even a Chinese or two,
Thousands of Spanish moriscos such as Ricote from Alcalá
Where I was born, Jews from Spain and Italy, from France and
The Levant, blue-robed Cypriot scholars, Corsican bankers,
Lawyers and doctors from Syria, traveling Rumis from God
Knows where, Moorish smithies, Hamite teachers, naked
Herdsmen of Kabyle, and, chief among these, the corsairs and
    their captives,
Most from Christian lands—French, Italian, Spanish, Rus

And English, Dutch, the Empire's men. Dali was Greek,
From the isle of Lesbos, his captain, Arnault, was Slav from the
    Adrian
Sea, the king of Algiers, Hassan Pasha, was Venetian,
And Agi Morato, the envoy, whose secret emissary I was,
Grew up on the Dalmatian coast. Christians and heretics,
Musulmen, Shiites or followers of Sunna, sectarian Jews,
Pagans, renegades or converts, those without religion,
All lived peacefully there,

                           Everyone had a story,
Wheels of fortune turning, how they fell, how they rose,
And all the twists between. Hassan Pasha, once Andrés
By name, was a cabin boy captured by Uldj Ali,
Who was so taken by his soft, hairless skin, his long, unformed
Thighs, that he became obsessed, mad with love, and, abandoning
His wives completely, was faithful to Andrés till death, poisoned
By his wives' relatives, some say, or squeezed between two boards.
Hassan Pasha remained a member of the tribe,
And he once told me he had never seen and never would
A woman whose flesh could charm him. At the battle of Lepanto,
He commanded a ship on the right of Ali Pasha's fleet,
Attacking the Venetian wing, where the Marquesa was deployed,
So we traded blows, it seems, though generosity has settled all
    scores.

Arnault Mami was a privateer long before his conversion,
Famed for kidnapping a Turkish grandee from the Pasha's court

And delivering him to Venice, it's an old-fashioned story
Of vengeance and honour, boring today, and I helped make
    it so,
But I would have used it, if death were not working like a
    mole.

On an expedition against the Turks, during the reign of
the Doge Gerolamo Priuli, some Venetians were taken
prisoners and presented to the Great Pasha. A bound
prisoner having said something offensive, one of the
Pasha's suite walked up and hit the Christian full-fisted
in the face. The prisoner, beside himself with pain and
indignation, cried out, "Rise up, O Venice, Gerolamo
Priuli has abandoned us, left us unprotected, allowed
the Turks to master land, sea, and honour."

Informed of this scene, the Doge felt humiliated, and
his anger worked on him at night like a bothersome
mosquito. He found his table lacking, closed himself off,
received no one, and, turning his chagrin into prepara-
tions, meditated upon his vengeance, which consisted
first in negotiating an exchange of prisoners, so that
the Venetian who'd been struck was bought back and
presented at the Doge's palace. The Doge showered gifts
and honors on the man and said, quietly, "We have not
abandoned you, nor forgotten you, and we have not
given the enemy either your blood or your honour."

He then had found in Manfredonia, along the rocky
Puglian coast, Arnault Mami, whom he knew preyed

upon the Turks like a white-headed osprey, and who spoke Greek and Turk and Arab. Gerolamo Priuli invited Arnault to court, locked himself away with him in oyster secrecy, told him his project, and asked him to help with all his ability and patience. After they agreed upon a plan, Arnault sent for Dali, who, having grown up in Lesbos, knew the Asian coast. He then spent a considerable amount of money buying rare and curious objects—tulle from France, Scottish and Flemish wool, Florentine marble inlays, Venetian colored glass, crystal bowls and goblets, furs of ermine and mink and otter from Moscow—while a boat of admirable construction, lighter than any other, was built.

Arnault set off, and, arriving at the island of Crete, saw the Beylerbey and told him that he had brought a young slave girl for the Great Ali Pasha, that he intended to trade with Constantinople, and that he wanted to deal with the Great Pasha and his court. Ali Pasha, informed by messenger of this man's desires, gave him leave to approach the capital, so the stranger was allowed to enter the mouth of the long channel that joins the Mediterranean with the Black Sea and soon docked at the city. In Constantinople, Arnault offered presents to the Pasha and his courtiers, but he purposely failed to give anything to the grandee who had struck the Venetian. When Arnault left for Venice, the Pasha and his grandees charged him with the purchase of many objects and merchandise that they specially desired from the west.

On arriving in Venice, he met with the Doge in secret and gave an account of his trip. He was furnished with the things he had been charged to buy and other objects he knew would flatter the Asian taste, and, in exchange, he gave the Doge cuttings from lilac trees of white and all the pale shades of blue, bulbs of the fragrantless tulipan, singles and doubles, in both pure colors of maroon, scarlet-orange, rose-carmine, pale violet, creamy yellow, deep brown, and bronze, and in broken colors, speckled or striped, like flame-streaked red or blue parrots, or pale yellow edged with green, and also a single bulb of a black iris. Gerolamo Priuli advised him, "On your next trip, the grandee will reproach you for your disdain and for not giving him presents. Make your excuses, soften him with attention, beguile his covetousness, enrich his pride, befriend his affection, and make him your patron and protector. Be sure to have him ask for something when you leave, and when you have faithfully executed my orders, when you know that the grandee is waiting for your return and for the commissions that he has given you, we will proceed to the next step."

Arnault then embarked for Constantinople, carrying everything he had been asked for and more that had not been asked for, which raised his position and his credit with the Pasha and his court. One day, while he was traversing the palace to reach the Pasha's apartments, he met the grandee, who stopped him and said,

"Have I offended you that you walk arm in arm with everyone else and laugh and banter, exchanging presents with them and taking their commissions, but me you totally ignore?"

Arnault bowed with a sweep of his wide sleeves and answered, "I am a foreigner, pasha, and have to be a mouse. I speak only when spoken to. I can only come to your country, to this city, pretending to be a prisoner or a spy, always fearful that my comings and goings will be noised about and denounced in Christian countries, which would mean death for me. But now that I know your sympathy, I put all my interests in your hands. I want you to speak for me before Ali Pasha and the others. Give me your orders, and tell me what I can bring you from the Christian countries." He then gave the grandee magnificent presents: a goblet of cut glass, perfumes, jewels, various antiques, rich woolen materials.

He and Dali continued in this way to come and go between the courts of Gerolamo Priuli and Ali Pasha, fulfilling commissions from the Pasha, the grandee, and other dignitaries. Meanwhile, the Doge dealt with the ravages of the plague that had recently arrived in Venice, carried by a trading vessel from the east; met with his ambassadors to the Council of Trent; and collected his bulbs. Several years went by without Arnault finding the right moment to execute the Doge's stratagem. Each time he came to Constantinople, he would anchor his swift little frigate near the grandee's home, a magnificent domain composed of a chateau and a splendid park that was situated on the banks of the straits, equidistant between Constantinople and the Black Sea. One day, while walking by the water, the grandee said to Arnault, who was preparing to return to Italy, "Would you be so good as to handle a commission from me? Could you buy me a painting of the kind for which the Italians are justly famed? I'd like it to be large and of different colors, red, blue, yellow, and aquamarine, and to have nude women in it and a frame that is elaborate and gold. The price is immaterial." Arnault agreed to this request.

Gerolamo Priuli, in a secret meeting with Arnault, heard all these details and procured a famous painting by Titian called "The Rape of Europa," soft, plump desire carried through the water on the back of a godly beast. Arnault took the painting and all the other products of Christian lands for which he had received commissions, along with instructions from the Doge on his stratagem and the means for success.

On his many voyages, Arnault had insinuated himself so well into the good graces and familiarity of the Turks that he was considered practically a compatriot, so much so that when, upon leaving the Mediterranean, he entered the straits under a favorable wind, he easily learned from the sailors of the ships and barges he encountered that the grandee was at home on his property. These straits connecting the two seas run some three hundred miles, and both banks were dotted with houses and estates. An incalculable number of boats and barges continually trafficked its waters, carrying all sorts of merchandise and provisions from various domains to the city and back.

Certain, now, that the grandee was at home, Arnault laid out the painting like a rug in an honorific arrangement on the deck, placing under deck his rowers, their oars in their hands but un-extended, as if lashed and stowed, so that no one would have supposed their presence under deck. The ship, its sails unfurled, shot up the straits like an arrow just released from a bow. No one on the bank could examine it, so rapid was its passing, so straight its course. She arrived in view of the chateau, where the grandee was indulging in festive pleasures with his harem on the belvedere overlooking the water. Excited by the intoxications of wine, he abandoned himself to expansive gaiety and joy. On seeing his friend's boat from Italy, he sang out a song of celebration and made everyone cheer its arrival. Meanwhile, the boat arrived below the chateau and furled its sails. The grandee, from his high vantage point, saw the painting laid out below, the beckoning flesh of Europa spread glistening like a bed of pale roses surrounded by the green-blue play of water, both real and painted. Unable to contain himself, he ran down even before all the others, climbing on board just as the captain stamped his heel on the quarterdeck, below which his men were hiding.

As soon as the signal was given, vigorous strokes carried the ship into the current, a heron's thrust, and she headed for the open sea without the slightest hesitation. Cries were raised, but no one could tell why, so rapidly had the whole thing happened. By the time night had fallen, the ship was already out of the canal and sailing freely in open waters, carrying away the tightly bound grandee. Wind and fortune favored her passage, and the ship crossed the extended sea. After seven days, she was in sight of the Italian coast, and by the thirteenth day, the prisoner was in the presence of Gerolamo the Doge, who allowed himself transports of joy upon seeing the success of his ruse. He called for the Venetian gentleman who'd been insulted to be brought to court. All the great men of the court convened and took their places; a large crowd pressed into the hall. Gerolamo Priuli, in crimson robes and wearing the embroidered cucurbit cap of state, addressed the Venetian, saying, "Arise and avenge yourself on this grandee who struck you in the face while you stood on the carpet before the Turkish chief. You see I have not abandoned you, have not given away your life or honor." As the Venetian rose and stepped up to the grandee, Gerolamo Priuli added, "But do not give more than you received. Avenge yourself to the extent of the affront. Do not give in to anger. Observe the law of retribution as God has prescribed."

The Venetian slapped his adversary several times and gave him a blow to the throat. Then he kneeled before the Doge, kissed his hands, and cried, "May Venice never lose you, defender of justice, protector of your subjects." And he continued to give thanks and praises.

Gerolamo Priuli treated the Turkish grandee with magnanimity, presenting him with apparel of honor, housing him generously, and giving him the painting by Titian as a gift, plus many other precious objects and presents for his King. "Return to your master," he said to him, "and say to him, 'I have allowed the Venetian Doge to render justice on your carpet and to avenge the injuries to which his subjects were submitted in your palace and before your throne of authority.'" Then, addressing Arnault, he commanded him to conduct the prisoner to the straits of Constantinople and leave him there along with all those who'd been captured with him, for several pages and followers of the grandee had boarded the ship with their master. They were taken to the ship amidst great fanfare and embarked. The crossing was easy. On the eleventh day, they entered Turkish waters and neared the mouth of the channel, which was closed with an iron chain and protected by a garrison. The grandee was landed with his companions, and Arnault and Dali returned home.

Upon arrival, the grandee took himself immediately to the Pasha along with all the presents and merchandise that he carried. The Turks celebrated his homecoming and congratulated him on his happy deliverance. The Ali Pasha was grateful to Gerolamo Priuli for the humanity he had shown the grandee, as well as for the gifts. Henceforth, while Gerolamo reigned, no Christian prisoner was ever mistreated. "Gerolamo Priuli," the Pasha said, "is the finest of Christians and very clever as well, which is why the Venetians chose him and gave him authority. Actually, if he wanted to kidnap me, I'm sure he would succeed."

Arnault returned to Puglia, to its deep lazuli waters,
Its secret, rocky coves and wet, rustling shingles,
And though he continued to war with the Turks, his
    friendship
With the grandee did not end. How he became a renegade,
Converted to the enemy's side, is a more modern kind of
Story I will never be able to tell, but will it
Surprise Your Excellency that Agi Morato was that grandee,
Whose son-in-law Arnault became?

How tempting to go on telling
The story, to cling to life in that desire,
To feel, perhaps, that a time will come
When I can take up the broken thread
And say what's left to say and what needs be said,
As if I joined the fated Sisters to spin out my own cloth
Or hide my me in stories so death can't find me out.

Ever housed in Libra, I go two ways at once,
Wanting to keep on writing, much as the rain keeps coming
   down,
But also to return to that resounding life,
As if Algiers were home, as I imagine it might have been,
The squawking parrots, the talking magpies,
The thrushes in shaded cages and clouds of coloured finches,
Knowing full well that only death can give me both,
Though without the jests, without comic or tragic,
Without irony. But perhaps the two, teller and tale
Are one, both delivered from the body of this life
Into the same eternity. I am my own story,
A striped cockle sewn to my hat, a gnarled staff in hand,
Cloth-wrapped feet and ankles, a pilgrim through my self,
Parched and dusty nettles on one side, shaded giant
Boulders on the other, as I thread through the ravine,
The red sand hills of Africa drifting into black
Pedregals in Andalusia at fall of day, swells
Of greyish olive trees surrounding me like the sea,
Tuscan hill towns embedded on stone promontories,
Sweet December orange blossoms enlargening the breath,
Stormy crossings, the cool fountains of Seville, dead dogs,
Flies on dung, the rain.

                    I dream of journeys repeatedly.
Yesterday was Easter. I said my last rites.
Tomorrow I go to Madrid, and by Sunday I'll be dead.

177

Though on this third day of April,
I'm still Your grateful servant,
In Esquivias,
M(iguel) de
cerb(an)tes.

THE EMPEROR'S 1619
LETTER TO CERVANTES

Dear Mi Hai,

I sway irregularly in my sedan chair, rocked to the heavy
breathing of porters. I know not if my letter will reach
you living or dead, but in any case I want to write you.
Drums rumble and echo off the canyon walls, a pulse
hidden in the shuffling of feet. The flutes sing above
willfully. I come to the sacred mountain north, a refuge,
to meditate the invisible beings of north, their powerful breaths heaving yellow loess through land and sky
or swirling hard, cold crystals to white, blind storms or
blowing parched gusts whose heat draws the body dry,
leaving behind thin, frangible locust shells of things.
These spirits reside here, unfriendly, foreign, at the edge

of center, beyond the great wall, facing the barren hills that Mongols worship, moving their unformed bodies slowly through crevasses and over peaks on this stony mountain that's always covered with rime-snow, howling and waiting for some human concern, which each year I give them, rites and repetitions, conformance, repeated fillings of empty containers, the ice-filled bronze *jian* with the cooling wine *fou* nestled inside it, the animal-like *he* pouring vessels, stone and bronze *jia* cups, the thin-waisted, gilded *gu* for heated wine, the *yi* for water, turquoise-inlaid bronze *pan* to receive the offerings, the double bronze *hu*, the *yü*, the *he*, each with its appointed wine, the winged *chi* for seeds, jade and bronze *xian*, *gue*, and *ding*, filled and emptied and filled again with millet and rice and sorghum and wheat, measured and re-measured, conforming the stuff of life to all these different, unique shapes and then emptying them again, not so much in sacrifice as in order to demonstrate our acquiescence to life as a constant filling of forms that have been given to us, the flowing of rivers or air, the filling of the bronze measuring bell we use to levy yearly taxes, the conformance of each to the other, much as we speak to or stroke one another, the hand to the body, the conforming and conjoining of male to female, female to male sexual members, of clouds to rain, not so much an appeasement as a way to locate these formless northern spirits by defining a boundary to centrality, and thus to offer them value and delineation in the formed world as a direction for us, since they trace our outer edge, a bare line, a circle defined by its center, defined not by prayer, since they can give us nothing, but by the declaration that they and we share in an equanimity that is the ground on top of which sorrows and pleasures, violence and gentleness, treachery and fidelity, evil and good, black dejection and red gaiety, gnawing hunger and sweating plenty, stubborn boredom and one-eyed enthusiasm play out throughout our lives. So I expect nothing from this yearly ritual, nor do I fear any disturbance if I don't observe it, for in reality, they are not beings, and certainly not fat gods or bulge-eyed spirits that can do anything. Yet insofar as they are our idea of what pre-exists the north-ness of north, which is itself no thing or being, yet which is a fact of our existence, they have powerful effects on our lives, though through no power that they can wield. For ten thousand years, emperors of the center have come to this source of turbid waters, to this temple amid the great, sandy hillocks that run miles down to the silted river, where my court now and for a week has awaited my arrival, for me to repeat the ceremonies that emperors have always performed here for no other reason than to give significance to order. But this is the first time I have come to the holy mountain itself, the first time I have left the palace, having always before performed the ceremony at the designated site within my secluded world.

This order that I acknowledge by meditating on invisible dwellers in the north can have little meaning for you; it hangs from a center that westerners do not admit. Your mapmakers say the world is laid out in four directions, as is the six-panel world map, made by the *hui-hui* Barndoor Li Madou, which hangs in my inner chambers, but without the direction of center, no world can be laid out. My north is someone else's south and my east is also west. Without a center, all is personal opinion, so western—or are they eastern—maps are like meandering lines that ceaselessly change without measure, without knowing the true direction of change, are random wanderings of continual extension, whereas here am I fixing the north absolutely by negotiating with these non-beings of Mount Heng. My equanimity depends on the fact of their non-existent presence in my life, depends also on my recognition of their factuality, for I could ignore their presence and only think of my life as a sequence of negotiations with the contingencies of reality, like a Chinese Quixote, but then, no matter how correctly I live my life, I would still always be subject to the doings of these non-beings, whose efficaciousness would seem to me, in my ignorance, chaotic and incomprehensible. As emperor, then, and not subject, I come to recognize their perilous state as determinations of the spatial realm in which I live. But even beyond the directions of space, Mi Hai, my space is very different from your space, considering, for example, that for you a cube and a square are different, whereas for me they are the same, but mostly considering that I measure my square so as to order my ethical life, whereas your space has no meaning and is only extension. What I do not like in a person whom I respect, I do not imitate for those by whom I am respected; what I hate in the person in front of me, I do not perpetuate upon the person behind me; what I hate in the person behind me, I do not perpetrate on the person in front; what I don't want to receive from the person on the right, I do not give to the person on the left; and, inversely, what I do not want to receive from the left, I do not give on the right. This way of measuring the square sets my center in an orderly complex of life; the earth, then, lays out a pattern of interrelationships among peoples, places, and countries; this lived geography provides meaning to the north, gives context for actions as a mesh of interacting differences between ourselves and others, recognizes the positions of others as well as our own, so that reciprocity creates our space, giving it a meaning that is sorely lacking in your notion of the golden rule, which only asserts your own self-interest as the focus of all willed action. As I explain myself to you, I find that I must constantly think in your terms and so lose my self, and this, I fear, is how your terms exert their inequality over mine. I am always interested in explaining myself to you, but you never feel the need to explain yourself to me, in my terms. Only the Jesuits do that, and theirs is a rhetoric for conversion.

Now I stop my palanquin here at the base of the sacred mountain itself, before this immense, black cliff that rises straight to the clouds and from which hangs an entire city, the monastery of emptiness. I can barely see the heads of my eunuchs and my officers of the guard as they cling to the cables holding the suspension bridge that leads from the lowest cave carved into the stone face a hundred feet above me out to the main reception pavilion that hangs over the sand, the rest of the monastery rising high above, with its columns, railings, beams, window frames, projecting eaves, niches, tiled roofs, and porticoes, the painted walls of its storied towers, its chambers and rooms, the sixty refectories and ten kitchens, the nine hundred meditation cells, one hundred and two reading halls, three hundred store houses, ninety-three dormitories, thirty-nine temples, and one thousand eight sanctuaries, all lit up by the afternoon sun, their red and green and gold hovering among crisscrossing scaffoldings of ladders and the shadows of ladders, illusionary stairs, hanging chain bridges or their traced imagery, suspended paths made of planks and supported by bars driven into stone or held solely by their mirages. I see them gesticulating and talking, some heads thrown back in laughter, some faces grimacing in shrieks. They point up and they point down, but their voices disappear into great emptiness.

Over a thousand years ago, the holy man Bodhidharma, he with one sandal, came here from Yindu and constructed this airy monastery, a center of the pure *dhyana* meditative school, constructed it to be an image of itself, ethereal, empty, one hand clapping or one sandal flying, site of his nine-year trance, yet busy ever since with the comings and goings of thousands of bikshus and shramans and arhats and bodhisattvas until, two hundred years ago, in the time of my great-great-grandfather Ming, the yellow-robed followers of Tsongkhapa moved here, their gongs, giant trumpets, bells, chantings, snapping banners, whirling prayer wheels, and clattering processional carts echoing daily off the black face of the cliff only to die across the sand hills, blocked by this stone mountain from rising up to the sacred northern peaks behind, which remain empty of all this human commotion.

The Buddhists try so hard to attain emptiness when it is all around them and within them. Why is it difficult to find that every idea is a pure emptiness, every story nothingness, color nowhere, line does not exist? Buddhists think that the crusty rocks and cloudy mountains, the dunning streams and myriad stars, the scented trees and birds that give pleasure, the animals and dragons and scaly beasts, the other people around us, all are real and visible, are easily available to us because of their reality, when, in fact, they are the most unattainable parts of our world. The world outside us is indeed real but mostly invisible and silent, empty, because we prefer to see and hear what we know and understand, conforming the real world to our empty selves. In this larger emptiness of our own creation, the difficulty is to pay attention to the little bit of non-emptiness we come upon and, by dwelling within that small spot of reality, filling the emptiness of our understanding, thereby realizing that external world we daily hide from ourselves. Our knowledge and understanding are empty because they are nothing more than the invisible scaffolding of our relationships arising to shape our lives. And whether the effect of this on us—on our knowledge and understanding, on our lives—be good or bad depends not on the nature of the people with whom we relate, whether enlightened or compassionate, not on what these people do or do not do, not even on their power to affect us, but rather depends on our differences, those hollow interstices between us where every relationship lives, whether between lovers or between a mother and son or between the governor of an island and his subjects or between a knight and his squire. And these differences—this airy scaffolding of relationships that widens and enmeshes with other relationships to form a huge country, all this invisible space and weather we live in—dictate our feelings and actions so that our individual choices or fates are of little consequence: are, in the end, but an illusion. I will forever be my mother's son, and she (though taught by the master De Qing, whose virtue is crystalline) could not speak to me but as to her son. Only in those moments when she does not recognize me can she forget her feelings as a mother, so that in those moments when she took me for her servant, she spoke to me as to a servant, so much are we controlled by our minds. When I told my mother that her mind was no longer secure, that she had to question what she thought to be true, she asked me what she could believe if she could not believe what she thought, to which I had no answer. A son will always feel pangs of resentment as he becomes a grown man, but when he faces his mother, he is again a son, and that separation within us, invisible and empty as it is, must nonetheless be made into another emptiness, that of understanding. De Qing the lucid, with whom I studied the Buddha's laws, discourses, and practices, who meditated on a bridge so that his inner silence could drown the noise of the waterfall, who forged his name on the imperial gift list so he could receive a copy of the Tripitaka from me, and whom I recently brought out of exile as a foot soldier in Guangdong, says that the first renunciation must be of the family, whose perpetuation is like a chain of karma, though karma itself is an uncertainty whose emptiness is based on the necessity of difference as we change from one life to the next, and all difference is factual, though, being the intervals of reality, none of it exists. Every relationship forms from many unknown and uncountable differences, so that a relationship between a rich person and a poor person, no matter who those persons are or how good they might be, will be fraught with hardship, a nail on which hangs kindness as well as cruelty, so that even if all differences in relative wealth were abolished, their other differences would persist, and so their relationship might not change, or change only imperceptibly, and so be just as difficult. In order for something to be given, it must be received, and since giving is not receiving, that difference, too, has its form, its scaffolding, invisible and empty, yet formulating on its own all such relations of giving and taking. Even though you are not my subject, our relation, too, rests like a bridge over the implacable difference between a son of heaven, a sky son, and a son of man, a difference as absolute as the difference between the middle kingdom and your country at the western edge.

All these scaffoldings, which make up our lives, stand outside of us and remain unaffected by our inner nothings; enlightenment does not affect them because they are the hollow ritual forms we are poured into and not our substance, which karma decants into one shape after another. For a thousand years, Buddhists have come and gone from this monastery, like the shadows that today have already disappeared into the dusky cliff-face, but these pavilions and caves and trellises have remained the same for whomever dwells here. The Yellow River floods some years and not others, whether the dragon who controls the waters is good or bad, loves the people or hates them, entertains ideas of power or of benevolence. Nature thus always remains nature, just as the north is always the north, an empty relationship to which our lives conform.

The ground is hard and impenetrable. It is the originating unity of *one*, which we represent by a horizontal line, to which we add the image of a man standing on it. We call this character *tu*, the earth. We stiffen our legs to stand on that ground, our bodies find support by resisting it, our muscles tighten to allow our bones to erect, and thus we, too, become objects, hard and impenetrable so as not to be of emptiness. At one year of age, we are introduced to this world of radical difference, of tottering, of falling against and into and onto painful solidity, we learn to survive like the monk Pumen negotiating the defiles of the City of Heaven on the Yellow Mountain, and we learn to succeed in life, scraping through the needle's-eye passages that run between the opening and closing chambers of the grottoes of Xü Xiake, and so we stand and walk and run on this hard earth, learning with each step that things are something and space is nothing, that we move by our own effort, that if our bodies are massive enough and hard enough, we can push things around, can move them by our own effort, and our self-confidence becomes jade. So, by the very experience of walking, we build our little world of illusions, thinking that we are self-sufficient, telling ourselves stories of heroes who command elements and circumstances and other humans, thinking, as we learn to walk, as we learn to not fall, that we are alone in the world, that we stand on our own two feet, that our space is discontinuous and full of discrete objects that are likewise self-supporting, separated from us and from all other things by a thin airiness, thinking that the more we hold our bodies rigid against the possibility of falling, our bodies ever straighter and more upright, the more we attain selfhood. That vacuous vapour surrounding the self makes all relationships act at a distance. This is the way of Adam, whose name I am told means "red earth."

But if I imagine we come from water, not earth, and if we can return to water, to that fluid space of continuous participation, then in water we would be supported by our own medium. Not only would the water move with us, but we would find our own bodies moving naturally in a balancing countermovement. In water, we cannot fall. We cannot push against water, stand on it, resist it. Water can thus be the figure for another type of space, where objects, like all growing things, cannot stand apart from one another, but are forever bound in proximate relationships, bound through and because of their immersion in water, even to the extent of losing identity. In such a world, seeing would be replaced by hearing, as observation would be replaced by sympathy, and we would discover that uprightness is all wrong and can only bring fear and death, for to live in water, we must float, and we can float only by giving ourselves to the water, by having faith in the full support of something that seems unsupportive because it gives way before us, because it conforms to all patterns without rigidity, because it is pure relationship without entity, because, indeed, we cannot sink, for only our desire for rigidity can drown us, and by living in water, we would not be burdened by a discreteness of self, a separateness that even the Pratyeka Buddha assumes, since the enlightenment he gains is a solitary experience, nor would we be burdened with the consequences of such discreteness, of our prideful insistence on effectiveness, of our assumption of a positive capability, of our preference for direct seeing. Yes, Mi Hai, water is a friendlier element, taking away the hardness that we think is reality, which is why Yesu taught the baptism of water. This is the way of yielding, *rang*, the copula of *yin* and *yang*, both male and female.

When the great Longmeng Pusa was living in an abandoned monastery that had been built into a cave, the young Pusa Dipo came to him from the country of Ji Size to beg a conversation on esoteric matters of wisdom. Longmeng sent his acolyte to him with a bowl of water. Dipo looked at the chipped bowl and dropped a needle into it, sending it back to the master, who shouted with delight upon seeing that Dipo knew the springs of action, an endowment far beyond the ability to penetrate subtle doctrine.

The great difficulty in life, Mi Hai, is to live in the flow of all these invisibilities which form our world and, when we find a speck of reality, to see it as nothing more than a grain of sand, to not let that grain overthrow our lives as a great revelation of the real. Don Quixote is overwhelmed by a world that is no more real than the one he creates for himself but whose claim to reality is indubitable because, whatever your true understanding might be, you, as author, support it, since, like a commitment to matter itself, you give tangibility more than its due. But I prefer the invisible beings of darkness to your passionate certainty of day. Yet, in your certainty, you are prophetic, for already the Jesuits are in my land, casting right and left their hard reality, which is nevertheless full of errors and illusions. Barndoor Li Madou spoke humbly, but he moved through space like a man who had conquered it, no water creature he. And how could a man who learned four hundred characters in an eye blink not feel certainty? How could he not cleave to the visible and reject the unknown?

It is something of a great historical irony, one that proves the unconcerned breathing in and breathing out of the complex and invisible relationships governing our lives, that I, a Han, say these things to you, a western Christian, since this doctrine of watery emptiness was preached by Yesu himself when he visited the central kingdom in his old age, though his teaching was itself a variation on those of the Buddhists of Kashmir, among whom he lived many years after surviving his ordeal on the cross.

In the darkened night, the Sky's Son steps out of his traveling chamber and orders sparklers brought. He holds a sputtering stick at arm's length, touching it to the one held by his consort, and the two stand, not moving, in the silver cascade that falls onto the sand around them like a nomad's dwelling until suddenly the whole sky is lit by bursting balls of fire and sparks that explode silently and just as suddenly slow their rotund expansion into a haunting stillness that clings to the dying light.

"I have pondered each one of Quixote's actions and find them all self-serving," he says aloud. Does he not choose freely and in joy to do everything himself, out of his own genial reasoning, through his own thorough understanding, for his own interests and desires, and to further his own goals? His Dulcinea is his own and no one else's. Ultimately, then, madness is selfhood itself, the self shorn of the external world of relationships. Ah, Mi Hai, you have made madness touching and humorous and appealing, and I foresee that day when your whole world will be mad, each person acting out of himself and for himself, raising free choice to a principle of life, assuming individuality as a structure of existence, reinterpreting your book of books to show that from the beginning of time, your god intended free choice to be the natural condition of man, Adam's and Eve's various discoveries of the delicate balances and changes and fates, whose windy scaffoldings shape primal human knowledge at the beginning of the book, turned into an exemplum of free choice, Paul's tintinnabulating rhetoric of anti-slavery near the end of the book turned into a demonstration of equalitarianism. All wisdom will be lost, Mi Hai, because all wisdom lies outside the self.

The ancient chronicles of the late Han dynasty end with the doings of foreigners from beyond the four directions who have come to the center. They tell of a white-robed Yesu dwelling in the snowy Kushana mountains of Kashmir at the great bend of the Yindu River, and of his journey west to Uddyana, whose king was a descendent of the daughter of a Naga dragon and one of the four exiled Sakya youths, cousins of Sakyamuni. Yesu was following the great expansion of Buddhism under Kanishka, king of Kushanas, into Bactriana and Turkestan, but he was not teaching the sacred texts, for he still considered his mission to be limited to the Jews, and he was following the traces of the lost tribe. He passed the Iron Gate, its giant bells still intact along the narrow defile, and descended into the fertile valley of the Oxus, turning north and east through Samarkand (which the local people said meant "fat") where the western melons grew so large that long-eared donkeys could only carry two at a time on their backs, the pomegranates reached the size of two fists, and grapes and pears were pressed into a delicious, thirst-quenching drink of a sour and sweet taste. The people there had thick beards like the Jews and the Samaritans, but their hair was entangled like sheep's wool and dyed black or yellow or orange. They used no utensils to eat with, tearing at their meat with their fingers and teeth. The women sang and danced all day long, and the men embroidered and sewed. He turned east through the White Mountains, where even in summer passes of snow and ice had to be cut with swords and hatchets. At the top of mountains were lakes in the middle of which, on islands, were great gatherings of birds, and near a city called Ah Li Ma, which is what the local people called *lin qin* trees, the trees grew so thick that no light entered. He ascended a high mountain that resembled a large rainbow overlooking an abyss of several thousand feet and was thrilled to look down upon a crystalline lake, into its very depths. At Su La he reached the desert of moving sands. He saw an eclipse of the blue-shadowed moon, passed ruined and abandoned cities, rolling hills of sand without end, without trees, picked his way through a battlefield of white bones. The desert people lived in black carts and white tents. Men and women both braided their hair long over their ears, and married women wore *gu-gu* hats two feet tall made of bark covered with wool or red-colored silk, behind which hung long tails like those of geese, and they would back into their tents to keep from having their hats knocked off. Thunder, lightning, wind, rain, sun, and moon followed their course, now hot, now cold. He passed grasslands with abundant water and salt lakes whose only life was a kind of tiny shrimp, until he arrived at last at the red sand caves of Dunhuang, where he learned from the monks that the Chinese were the lost tribe of Jews, though after two thousand of years of intermarriage, we had ceased to look Jewish. At Dunhuang, Yesu began preaching, and for eighteen years he wandered the central kingdom as a beggar and pilgrim, accompanied by a tame deer and carrying a gourd of water and an iron staff, for he was lame because of his crucifixion. He preached and he cured with water, achieving great fame among Taoist alchemists and exorcists, and is today still revered as one of the eight immortals under the name Li Tieguai. When he was very old, in his seventies, and thought he could not live longer, he returned to Kashmir with some of his disciples and was buried there, not far from the tomb of his mother, Mary, who had accompanied him to Kushanas in his flight from Jerusalem.

I expected to find this same story in your book of books, but there I found speech doubled, the evangelists so interested in selling religion—as if religious beliefs were concocted and not natural—and in creating a church, that instead of speaking out of the entanglement of a mind grasping diligently at its own ideas, like Taoist texts or Buddhist sutras or any of the Five Classics, your New Testament, so characteristically western, both tells the story of Yesu and turns that story into a commodity, overlaying it with the intent and salesmanship of the merchant. So, although Yesu cured the sick out of compassion and not, as he himself said, to give miraculous signs, the evangelists present his works as miracles. He spoke in parables and saw no need to explain those mysterious truths, but the evangelists, being rhetoricians, put explanations into his mouth, explanations that deny his mysterious perceptions. Yesu never intended to preach a new religion, never intended to minister to non-Jews, for he said many times, *Do not go to the Gentiles or the Samaritans but only to the lost sheep of Israel, salvation is of the Jews,* and acted thus pointedly, refusing to help the Samaritan mother and calling non-Jews dogs and other nasty names. But the evangelists, wanting to create a religion among the Gentiles, their own people, add a later injunction to preach to the whole world, though even this interpolation is belied by the story that when Paul asked to preach with the disciples, he was sent off to the non-Jews while the disciples reserved the Jewish mission for themselves, so clearly Yesu never sent his disciples out to the ends of the world, or if he did, they did not understand him, and if they did not hear or understand him, then I wonder how the evangelists heard it. In the same way, your evangels obfuscated Yesu's death and resurrection with layers of ambiguous suggestion, advertising their new religion like a sleight-of-hand attraction, like puppet-show singers clashing their cymbals. Yesu spoke of resurrection as an afterlife, a reemergence in Heaven as a living being, and never as kicking stones on the paths of this life.

When stripped of evangelical intention and the rigidity of doctrine, when understood, instead, and as Yesu taught, as the fluid conformance, or *rang*, of wind to earth, of light to water, of dark to air in the ever-changing swirl of fate, the story of Yesu's supposed death reveals a simple drama. He was crucified, as Mark tells it, at nine o'clock in the morning and fell into a swoon at three in the afternoon, when the eclipse passed, but crucifixion, a cruel and slow death, takes much longer than six hours, usually requiring several days to kill a man, and so even Pilate was surprised when Joseph of Arimathaea asked for Yesu's body in the early evening, which is why he sent for the centurion in charge of the crucifixion. The centurion, whom both Matthew and Mark say was a sympathizer, reported that Yesu was "without life," an ambiguous phrase. But Pilate, who had never wanted to crucify Yesu in the first place, and who felt he had been forced to go through with the death penalty to satisfy the demands of the Jews, now understood that the centurion's ambiguity gave him a way to wash his hands of Yesu's death, so he gave Joseph permission to take Yesu down from the cross, which was done, his wounds anointed with sarcocol and other healing herbs and balms provided by Nicodemus and bandaged in linen, and then he was hidden in a cave behind Joseph's house. Three days later, much to the consternation of Mary Magdalene and Joanna and Mary, mother of James, as well as the others who were caring for him, Yesu left his place of hiding. He hobbled with the help of a staff, which made Mary Magdalene take him for a gardener with a shovel, and both he and his abettors said that he had arisen from bed, not that he'd been resurrected from the dead, that he felt strong enough to walk, that he had many things to do, and that he was alive and fine. He was seen by Cleopas and several of the watch, all of whom attested to his corporeal presence, and he made his way to his disciples, to whom, and especially to Thomas, he again affirmed his being alive, even asking for food to demonstrate his earthly condition. Since he knew that his life was in danger from the Jews as well as from the Romans, he separated himself from his disciples, and, helped by his silent mother and Thomas, the doubter, he went east.

What Yesu did in Yindu and the central kingdom—his teachings, the absorption of Buddhism into his watery theme, the receptivity of the invisible—were subjects of no interest to the new religion of Paul and

Peter in the west, which based itself on the certitude of the church, and so the Jesuits themselves are still even now in a quandary over their discovery in southern Yindu of the tomb of Thomas and the congregations of Yesu's and Thomas's followers, and Barndoor Li never believed that Yesu's and Mary's tombs are in northern Yindu and have been worshipped there by both the Musulman and the Buddhists for seventeen hundred years. Yet you come to convert us.

The tents pitched and the cauldrons boiling, the Ancestor, slowly and with difficulty, walks in the dark, two feet together, left, right, together, at Yü's pace, marking in the sand the seven-foot alternation of male and female so that he trails behind him, in groups of three, the nine prints of the sixty-third hexagram (*jiji*, beyond completion) wherein all elements are in their place: a power walk of protection used to enter the wilds where spirits dwell, and so also a walk teetering on danger.

Completion is only an ordering of a beginning. Your book of books and our book of books, the *Yijing*, first among Classics, both begin with the beginning of things, but we write a single horizontal line in a single stroke, while you weave yourselves into a story of will, decision, action, and desired and determined consequence, a process that transforms a primal actor's will into birds and trees and rocks according to the varying dramatic tensions of narrative inevitability. Our single solid line, which is no allegory but rather the simple representation of unity, is *one*, both as the initial solid line of the hexagrams of change and as the character for the number one. That unity, though, once formed, enters into the progress of becoming two, its existence at once implying a distinction between some thing and the nothing around it, dividing above from below, before from after, thus creating two from its own singular nature. So unity is not rigid and fixed but rather moving (that is, changing through opposition), and, since movement is straight, and thus the male, the father, the thrust, the one is received by the two into which the one proceeds, received by the opening formed between the one and the one when the single line is opened into two lines to represent the duality of the one, thus changing the male into the female, which, too, is unfixed and proceeding, the one and the two together, giving and receiving, making three marks, which we call *qian*, the sky, the father, suggesting the chariot wheels of continuance and a human being and the sequence of one and one and one, suggesting also the three females of *kun*, the image of the earth and fields, so that we represent creation not as solid stuff but as just the nature of being, which is no more and no less than changing forms. But you have a god who wills, acts, and determines the consequences of his actions as he is willing them, thus establishing the rule of efficacy—though where he comes from we do not know. And so each and every one of you, even the mad

Quixote, thinks life and existence are just that: choice, action, and consequence played out on a field of unfeeling matter. I heard this assumption of efficacy in the talk of Barndoor Li—decisions, action, aims, what can be done, what are the effects, do this and that happens, but if we do that, we can get this done—and when I studied your language, how astonished I was to find that everything you say can only be said in the image of your god's efficacy. In your tongue, an agent acts upon an object, so that with every utterance you repeat your original aberration—*let there be light, I make light, you make light, he and we make light*—and there can be no other sense and meaning in your talk. You are all little gods. We are all little people, getting by in a changing world as best we can, contemplating one separate word at a time, but you will and determine and think you control consequences. You judge a ruler bad if his decisions have brought his dynasty to an end, you will judge me thus, but who dares say what has caused what? Every act has ten thousand causes and ten thousand effects, but your god demonstrates and your grammar proposes one cause and one effect.

And so, Yesu, lame, hobbled by his notion that he was the son of god, unable to leave god in his allegorical world, had to insist that he was the lightning rod of god's will on earth, making that will descend and search out every shadowed crevice of human consciousness, making everyone in turn exercise their own little will and determination, making a meddlesome god, stricken men, and all life evangelical: an epidemical madness that no cinnabar or gold or orpiment, no night glowing excrescences, no avoidance of starches, can cure. Once imagined, your god's will cannot be denied; we will ourselves to ask for it. Already the Jesuits teach that god's purpose in creation was the Christianizing of the whole world, so that the stony reality your god created alone constitutes what is certain for you, what you see, hear, touch, taste, smell, differing from all other things of which you might know or be conscious, and this certainty is an existence to which you are attracted, committed, attached, and by which you are persuaded to measure all else, so that you cannot imagine a fabulous world without imagining it fabled, not real, no matter what magical or logical games you play when thinking about it (what if we dream that we dream that we dream), that presence of substance which is certainty itself now for us, too, imbued with the will to complete itself by our conversion. Certainty of presence, with its Christianizing intent, is the bedrock on which you build your knowledge, and even though the present is ever changing, ambiguous, and drifting, a certain corporeality has begun its ascendance in the world. All this energy tires me.

The Wanli Emperor sees his world changing—though through no action or inaction of his own. His laxity, his illness that would not allow him to engage in the world, his comfort with uncertain detachment, all this gave him a sense of perseverance and endurance in calamity but provided him no aim, no goal, no ideology for that endurance, no certainty that what is real is real. And so his world drifts in that strange, amalgamated condition of changes in which anything and everything happens normally. To some it may seem a world without time, without physical reality. Reading Cervantes, Shen Zong could not be other than tired, for Don Quixote moves in a field of energy that swells out from the certainty of reality. And perhaps that is why Don Quixote, too, unable to find detachment, is himself tired throughout the *Second Part*. When Don Quixote attacks the windmills, there is no doubt that the windmills are windmills or that Don Quixote lives in the aberrations of his mind, no matter the emperor's sympathies. The windmills do not lift themselves up into the sky to avoid Don Quixote's lance, which has not grown immensely into a golden scythe large enough to slice them through—the Wanli Emperor wonders why not. But in the *Second Part*, Don Quixote faces actors and puppets, the machinations of the Duke and Duchess, the disguises of Carrasco, and is tired of all these games of illusion, which still take place in that too-solid world whose certainty he wants to unlearn. The emperor is tired by the premonition of his own decay. It was his glands, though some say he was addicted to opium.

The emperor slumps like one of the crushed cushions that support him as servers lay out his evening meal on the large table in front of him. The white silk walls of the tent magnify the hardly noticeable swaying of the lanterns, which shoot reflections wildly about. He sits alone, eyeing the dishes as the uncovering of each one allows a small, vaporous cloud to burst out. Every dish is described by the eunuch in charge, its place of origin explained. The emperor's eating ritual is the most primitive of all imperial rites. It was for this that the empire had been formed thousands of years ago: to ensure the feeding of the intermediary between sky and earth. Earth was only *land* when it grew food; the rest—the woods and mountains and deserts— might be cast to the spirits or to robbers, monks, and artists, who had no civil interest, but this human land was entrusted to those who worked it, who sent its food to the emperor's table, and, bound always by this obligation to that land, they were never permitted to sell it except by temporary mortgage. Laws of taxation were joined to laws of inheritance so that a family could never divide their land into ever smaller and thus less productive parcels; appendices were added to deal with lands washed away by floods as well as those formed by the eel-like movements of rivers—all so that every bit of land would produce food for the emperor's body, glutinous rice being the adhesive between earth and sky. The mores of Confucian family ethics fertilized a family's rooting to the land, to the place where their ancestors were buried, where altars were maintained with the nightsoil of worship, obligation, and virtue— all for the emperor's table.

The emperor sits over a map of his lands, every province represented by a dish of food—gelatined beef hooves from Sichuan, crocus and phalarope feet from Hebei, swallow mucilage with fungi from Guangxi, preserved pea sarpamenta from Guizhou, monkey's brain and palm hearts from Annan, the black-nosed dace of Huguang, fern fronds, black radishes, preserved saxicolous melons and scabrous roots, cheeses of grain and phaseolus noodles, the crumpled yellow gyromitra of Shenxi, the striped bulimus, variegated helmets, Nanan spinach—every dish a combination of ingredients from water, earth, and sky, each designed to demonstrate an alchemy of place. The emperor takes from every dish, and, with each bite, validates not only the food's laborious past but also the longer tale of self-righteous laws and habituated customs that leaps out every evening in the tastes and textures of his meal.

There is no exotic question of pleasure in this, for, being the place where sky meets earth, the emperor could hardly be expected to develop personality or individual feelings apart from idiosyncratic and thus inconsequential ticks of identity, and I do not aspire to anything else. He is not a Caesar, not even your Felipe, but rather an abstract location, a center for this table setting of sustenance. Though the Da Ming was founded by a powerful warlord who usurped the position of emperor, I myself was merely born into this position, and so am here to function—only for a while, not everlastingly, though I have reigned longer than any other emperor—until I die, until ousted, my family replaced by another in the endless procession of form that is life. Personality is not warranted and has proved, repeatedly, destructive. Even these looming cliffs now appropriately vanished in the darkness seem an abstraction of location rather than a geographic point, since, leaving the secluded city for the first time, I find myself still the center here at the root of sacred north, so place has a moving quality, too. Nor can this abstraction be identified with the emperor himself or with his family, so frail were both his health and that of his dynasty. That curious conceit the Jesuits had explained to him, which described the great architectural monuments of the west as eternal objectifications and permanent memorials of the individual personalities of their creators, as if people did not die, rock did not crumble, and wood did not burn, seemed to him not just laughable but so utterly stupid, so incomprehensible and ignorant, that these people seemed from another world entirely. Perhaps you have machines to measure and count time because, without these turning wheels and ornate fingers, you would be lost in the flux of life. Perhaps, as my mother did in the last years of her life, you forget everything. When Barndoor Li first stood on the dragon pavement at the axis of the world, he felt depressed at the inhumanity of the place, its lack of character, its impermanence. It seemed a place of bizarre, passing fancy, chilled and passionless for all the debauchery we were said to indulge in, and not a place for virtuous men of power. He was depressed by the green weed lines growing up between the marble slabs, the bits of broken red plaster coming off the walls, was overpowered by the dull red gold work and tarnished silver, the heaviness of our timbers and the gaudiness of our lacquer, and I think he remained ignorant of why we feel entirely comfortable with cranes and demons, sneering lions, writhing dragons and chickens.

At my age, which I so clearly remember once thinking to be the age of wisdom, I am no nearer to understanding whatever purpose might guide those complex relations between people that people everyone's lives than I was then; in that still, clear memory, I thought that someone half my present age would, should, surely have lived enough, fulfilled enough of a life of possibilities to readily and willingly depart. And yet I have long surpassed that age without ever knowing that sufficiency or even that expectancy. Even now, the smallest of disturbances seems an overwhelming subject of would-haves and could-have-beens, that so intertwine with the events as they happened that no past is possible except as a rhetoric of the present, mixed together with those eternal truths that I have gleaned from others in order to make the future possible. Perhaps that is why I write you, Mi Hai. Ever since the Barndoor came to the central kingdom, I have seen that our worlds will someday be one, and in the four seas of that future, Don Quixote and I seem related.

So be it.

I.

THE EMPEROR'S 1620
LETTER TO CERVANTES

Dear Mi Hai,

I am entombed in my own body. The emperor sits in silent darkness at three in the morning. In the time of the Grand Secretary Zhang Juzheng, Han Feizi invented a cylindrical casing armed with needles all around pointing inward, and to punish the inventor for his cruel imagination and to test the torture chamber, the emperor ordered him placed in one of his own instruments. Han Feizi asked his keepers for a brush and paper and wrote a poem to the emperor. *Such is the path we follow, / between evening and the next day, / that we seem playthings of a dream. / Stop shivering, have patience; / thousand-armed fate strikes one family after another.* That day the emperor was busy and laid the message aside without reading it. The next day, he read the poem and ordered Han Feizi released from his chamber, but the inventor was already dead. He had been in the cylinder forty days. I have been longer in mine, and yet in some strange way, the bloated, blotched, unrecognizable flesh that surrounds me seems there only in order to turn upon itself: to feed itself its daily doses of pain so that I feel it only in the body, an alien sensation, while my mind remains untouched, like the shying net of light at the clear water's bottom. Only when the pain rises to his head does its undertow sweep his thoughts swirling into its pulsing on-rush, and then he thinks only of the pain and its infinite, delicately nuanced furies. But tonight, in the silence that is pulled over his eyes like a tight robe over his head, only his gigantic feet and melon hands ache. Who created thought, this wonderful plea-sure whose feelings, images, and narratives are not his, are not in him but flow through him, unwilled, seem, in the passage through him and others, to bind them together in an unspoken relationship, since his thoughts, which arise by themselves to his conscious-ness, always open into an aura of commonness rather than into singularity? Not your god, who only created things. Is thought something we invented ourselves, like speech, though, unlike speech, always unreliable, invented to be true to ourselves, but which we squander by speaking? He drifts into an image he feels in his hand of making a checklist and marking off each item with a small, circular movement of his brush tip. The items are essential to the settlement of a conflict, and that importance seems a large crystal *xüan ji* astronomical clock made of gossamer-thin gears that flash lines of rainbow color in the emptiness, each glass wheel representing fights and arguments, rising tempers, angry and disdainful rebuttals, prideful shovings and hair pullings, mindless beatings caused by Wei Siyong in a village, but the moment he remembers Wei Siyong's violence his thought vanishes, for the case was at least forty years ago, and he never made such a checklist, since the judgment was rendered without his intervention and was only told to him, one of tens of thousands of such incidents he has listened to and cast out of his mind. Losing that thought, he feels disappointment, its simplicity without doubt, his anxiety or question now replaced by memory and time and multiple considerations: the realization that for months his hand, engorged and lifeless, could not hold a brush, the wonder that this irrelevant case remained in his mind and that even the criminal's name returned to him. Pure thought—not the inner speaking to himself that passes for thinking, nor the deliberate recall of the past, but rather thought in its unbidden self—is like that, simple and without anxiety, like dreams, is a dream that continues in my inner, not outer, mind, day and night, always there but hidden much of the waking hours by the discrete curtain of language. Thought is finding on the ground a single, brown scroll leaning cockeyed against the cobwebbed wall of a dusty storeroom and knowing, without hesitation, that here is the voluminous biography of that murderer become monk who was his father but who did not look like him, who looked instead like the scribe, though he knew without looking that the man was his father, whose *Huang Ting* canon of the physiology of the spleen, written in magical, seven-character lines, I had sought or was still seeking in the grotto by the stone bridge after his disappearance. Thought is watching from the red tower through the hemlocks, fir trees, and bay laurels, an image distinct from but becoming continuous with looking down at a crowd of old women dressed in the ancient style, though their clothing suddenly appears more ragged than ancient, refugees from another year who shout in a language I do not understand but think I might at one time have learned and forgotten. In the progressing change of thought, those hemlocks, fir trees, and bay laurels now seem much smaller, held as disguises by a squadron of soldiers, whose faces he could now see were painted like wide-mouthed demons as he runs with them, advancing surreptitiously across the square, stopping and kneeling now and then to pretend to be a grove of trees, watched by him in horror and indignation as the trees swooped upon the old women to the clashings of gongs and drums and then disappeared, having devoured the women completely. Thought is that ease of being watcher and doer without distinction, is that equanimity of knowing passion and fear and emotion, is the bath of all events experienced as a single immersion without discreteness of then and now or might have been and would be, is a world where Zhang Juzheng looks like Fat Feng but is still Zhang himself, where the shadowed side of my face can be a terrace of orchids and summer bamboo, a strong man walking. And thought is pure because untrammeled by sensations, undaunted by the sun's clinging brightness, by the hardness of things and the incessant identities of sound, pure because in thought touch is the irides-cent blue he wears or the pale, light yellow that shades into the throaty whisper of a dove heard from far away, so forms of thought, its storied images, stay ambiguous, changing, copulating to rise now and then into the this-is-this-and-not-that of language, into its I-am-me-and-you-are-you, its then-and-not-nowness, arise as ideas or metaphors, violating discretion, and so, like relics, are useful only as objects of contemplation and dismay. Thought is what he is left with after his body abandons him to follow its own path to death, and he discovers then that thought's cavernous openings are the most ancient part of himself, the most distinctly primordial and central, yet, because shorn of will, desire, and intent, also the most selfless. In thought he is everything, everywhere, and every person, so he shares and is shared with every thought, which seems a secret act of love or understanding. You and he, Mi Hai, even after death, share thought: not speech, which we translate back and forth between languages, never getting it right, but eyeless and earless thought, through which we share those feelings that remain undirected, feelings that, void of self-interest, are nothing other than the fragrance that all thoughts bloom into, not like flowers but like herbs in a darkened, wood-paneled room, the dry, pungent aroma of an herbalist's shop. Large sheets of paper are laid out on the red, polished countertop. Shriveled fungi, dried twigs, and twisted roots, turned slowly in the hand and examined in the dim light, fling their concentrated powers into the air like spores. Seen close up, the sheets of paper become pages of a small book. Thus the feathered edge of his thought, like a line, hugs the shore of things; in thought he is most expansive, and so most emperor, most son of the sky. Never acting for his own sake, never speaking for himself, always waited on, he cannot but trust others, so that in thought I am also most human. But thoughts pass and pass, an image of loss itself. Enemy to language and to sensation, thought is also enemy to memory. He cannot keep thought from disappearing, its invisibility vanishing when unnoticed, and, noting how it shatters silently into the shards cupped in his hands, he has no means, certainly not memory, to restore the cup, for we live by opiate forgetting. If every slant of a goose's wing, every soft turning of a page, every fall of sweet oranges to the ground, were not instantly forgotten, the total stillness of all-at-once would overwhelm him, the goose tumbling unseen from the sky, the page lie unread, the apomictic orange seeds unscattered on the ground. We forget to be able to live, there's no other way, so his thought's passing is his most unmediated sense of living, of a self that loss makes possible, and perhaps is all there is of life. And if that were so, he might think death an obsession held, a thought that does not desist, a conquering, meddlesome, and insidious tyrant, a Qin Shi Huangdi, not the calm darkness of sleep but sitting awake in the night tatting the same thought over and over until it replicates like the grotesqueries of nature that people always bring to show him, two-headed peacocks, a cricket the size of a rat, a girl with three breasts, where some natural part insists on overdoing itself and does not stop growing, though who can know what death is, knowing never comprehending unknowing. Even such clinging thoughts have their own pleasure and equanimity, for the anxiety that accompanies them is more a worrying of the will than a quality of the thoughts themselves, which remain carefree in their tyrannical curiosity. Is he already dead? The hillside is steeply carved by rivulets of gravel and stone so that the boulders lodged on the sides of the gorges form small shelters, under one of which the villagers show him a sitting bodhisattva, his caftan in colorless tatters, his whole face sinking into his skull, the thin, dusty pergamon that covers his skeletal figure breaking in those places where the curious push their doubting fingers, and since he is still sitting, the villagers consider him still to be meditating and thus immortal. His question is like his mother's problem. Only on the threshold between two minds do the sane distinguish themselves from the demented; otherwise they are much the same. If his thought persists, and as long as his thought persists, refusing to pass into the nothingness out of which his memory might or might not call it again, he is unable to know if he is dead or merely thinking, and, if thinking, if he is thinking sanely or insanely, having nothing else to trust but this recycling thought as it recycles itself, since he is, indeed, this very thought and no stand-apart watcher. He is dead and cannot even know that he was dead many times before. He waits then for a last memory by which he will know the passing of thought from its disembodied absence. He waits cautiously because his thought is a long thread that trails behind him, leading back into an enormous tangle that threatens to tighten into a massive knot if he were to turn away and pull on it, but in the dark he is unable to carry his end of the thread backwards through the unseen, looped windings, though he is feeling his way inch by inch, undoing the thoughts of a lifetime, now seemingly all one single thought, unable also because he cannot undo by himself what he has not himself made, what was done by everyone together with him. A leopard spider with red flanks hangs upside down, clinging to the web's center, waiting tentatively for prey, but he brushes the web aside with his sword, though it remains intact, the spider not even moving as, trussed under the arms, he is lowered past the web, past the thorn and fig bushes, into Montesino's cave, and though he expects to catch and knock against the rocky sides, he finds the descent smooth and harmless, his body weightless against the rope. In Java, a black and curly-haired pearl diver is pulled up from the monstered deep and wrapped in thick, steaming cloths. East of Java, he remembers, is a land of women. The stooped scribe bends over his writing lit by a single candle, and he pulls the red lacquered brush towards his caved-in chest in short bursts of irregular rhythms. He is not dead, but sits watching the scribe record his thoughts. Quixote's is the saddest story I know because he is a harmless, innocent, good and wise man with Li Zhi's *child's heart*, brought down not by fate, not by his own actions or flaws, not by accidents of occurrence, not even by the treacherous deeds of evil people, but by being held to a sanctimonious norm of right behaviour by those indecorous, censorious people who themselves do not live by what they shout so loudly when in public. He presses his forehead to the gritted paving stone while the actors sing out the scene of his drunkenness as directed by his mother, the slave girl whom he'd struck playing her own whining role, his part played by a fat, waddling eunuch with his face painted lasciviously in red and black. Between each repetition of the story, the whole assembled court calls out to him, *ren yi li zhi xin*, the five Confucian virtues, the cant of public life. The square completes itself as if he has brought his forefingers and thumbs together, slowly raising his hands thus joined into the air, a pearl diver rising to the surface, ears and nose plugged with wax, sometimes with horrible gashes in his side or missing a leg. The diver, teeth clenched, is black and has curly hair, but he is Li Zhi, who hangs himself when the emperor condemns him for impiety. He thinks, "This cannot be because Li Zhi died a long time ago," but the thought, like snow that will not settle, moves lightly on with his disquiet sifting away under it. The diver is a thought that reaches for Ge Aile's breast with small, outstretched hands that do not reach higher than her waist. The nipple is erect. If he could suckle it, the thought would settle and leak out its cold, but he cannot reach it. A childish desire that never finds satisfaction, thought passes from one longing to another, rising again and again to the waving arms of light, seeking only a small jerk of comfort. But he feels the line tug on him from below. It is tangled below him in the waving, dark kelp, and, surprised at his own fearlessness, he descends to retrace the thread of his thought. Sunlight drills into the scrubbed, green sea, winking all around the diver as he lets out his last air through clenched teeth. The small bubbles tickle past his face in their rush to rise. Changxün's small body settles into a new comfort as he shifts position and lets go of the nurse's nipple. The nipple is erect, enlarged and surrounded by erected flesh, aroused further by the sudden touch of cold. He wants to caress her nipple, to lick away the small stream of milk that bubbles across her breast when Changxün releases his hold on her, to suckle her and share the milk that she gave to Changxün, but he dares not follow his desire, dares not follow the path of inner *yin* that the eccentric Li Zhi preaches, dares not reach his hand out to stop her hooking her dress over her warm breast, because of impropriety, because though he believes that all true distinctions are distinctions of *yin*, he also knows that no intention, no inner thought, is understandable in the outer world of *yang*, so that to reach out his hand will always be improper, whatever his feelings and thoughts, and so his longing stays within him as a thought held, a swirl of light snow that slowly settles to release underneath the coldness of propriety. The curly-haired, black diver descends, following his line into the dark. He is Zou Yüanbiao, whose ripped and swollen back, sides, and flanks turn purple and black from being beaten with bamboo rods, yet who returns from exile to publicly reprimand once more the emperor's improper conduct. The emperor says *so be it*. It cannot be heard but is echoed and amplified by two, then four, then eight, and finally by the thousand voices of his blue-robed guards who are ranged along the four walls of the courtyard. Thought is a square that completes itself, the urgency gone. The punishment continues. He knows that Zou Yüanbiao is a person of *yang* who only memorializes the emperor to be recorded in history as a moral man, unlike the sincere master Li Zhi, but Zou's willingness to risk pain, mutilation, and death for the *yang* of sanctimony impresses his sullen mind, and he knows that he must finally acquiesce to the piety of Confucian virtues, though he leaks that cold acquiescence silently into his life. Not as harmless nor as innocent nor as good and wise a person as Quixote, yet he, too, is borne down through no fault of his own, victim neither to fate nor to evil plots, borne down solely by the insistent weight of right behaviour. Like a spider, the scribe eases himself down the thread of ink that flows behind the smooth turns and tucks of his moving brush tip, the descent smooth and harmless, his body weightless, until he finds a ledge on the side of the cave where he rests and draws in the rope behind him. He turns to find the ledge opening into a grove of bernecla trees, partridges hanging pear-like from short stems. Montesino, dressed in weeds like a Taoist monk, walks towards him holding out Li Zhi's heart wrapped in an embroidered cloth. The emperor's eyeless thought tries to follow the strands of embroidery in the cloth as Changxün, who is Montesino and has grown a beard like a westerner, unwraps the heart, showing him a dark, shriveled thing in his hand; it is puckered and hard-ridged, like something in an herbalist's shop. He turns it slowly in the dim light of the wood-paneled room. It is his thought, and it does not move. It is dead, pulled tight and knotted into this hard lump. He wants to cut the threads with his sword but is afraid to, and so he cautiously feels his way, inch by inch, backwards along the unseen looped windings, undoing the thoughts of a lifetime, now pulled tight into a single thought, but he moves tentatively and fearfully because he does not want to break the thread that trails behind him still. His death is an obsessive thought from which he can be released only if he unravels all those ideas and images and stories, which were never his to begin with, which he had read and heard, and which grew out of his relations to everyone and everything, which tied him to the world's apparencies. And so his mother's swollen, arthritic fingers peck at tiny, incessant loops of thread, enlargening some, tightening others, pulling over and under and through. She fumbles but works steadily without pause in the sunlight. Her small stool in the courtyard is surrounded by an enormous mat of tangled thread that grows larger as she works, senseless to time, which is reckoned overhead by the thudding of the ravens' wings. Persistent as a parched cadaver, paper-thin, her yellow skin clinging tightly to her skeleton, she refuses to pass on. She is a follower of *dhyana* and a student of De Qing, meditating the wall in front and the waterfalls below. The hillside is steeply carved by rivulets of gravel and stone so that the boulders lodged into the sides of the ravines form small shelters, in one of which the villagers show him a sitting bodhisattva, the whole face sinking into the skull, his colorless caftan in tatters, his thin, dusty pergamon covering his skeleton broken in those places where the curious have pushed their doubting fingers, and since he is still sitting, the villagers consider him still to be meditating, and thus immortal. The emperor's thought does not move. It is the skull of a hydroencephalic child enlarged threefold. It is a two-headed calf. It is the tyrannical curiosity of nature or the cancerous obsession of powerful men, Qin Shi Huangdi building the great wall and burying a whole army of clay soldiers, horses, and chariots. He does not forget his thought, does not feel it slipping underneath him into some dark and unknown past, does not feel himself as a capacity to recall a past that his forgetfulness creates. Witless, he watches the tattered raven tumble from the sky, falling never to land, falling but unfallen. He holds its invisible body cupped in his hands to examine it carefully. Is it dead? In the dark, he tats its feathered edge, waiting for a resurgence. If thought is where he loses himself into the expansive everywhere, then is the stopping of thought a gaining of self, of separateness, of singularity? In death, then, he stops being emperor, stops being the son of sky, a ritual of humanity who never speaks his thoughts, who never acts for his own sake; he stops being human and becomes simply himself, alone on the shoreline of things, just another thing. In death, without the quick of thought, he shares nothing with Mi Hai or with Changxün, nothing but the dusty prevarications of language, its hieratic grammars of self-importance, of will and desire and intent. In death, he is a plaything of words, of their distinctions and separateness, of their discretions. His thought does not fall away but turns upon itself like a palindrome. Senseless, he hears the distant call of the mourning dove fading into faded, light yellow caresses on the palaces of his face. He can see the gongs and drums that announce his entrance into the hall of public meeting, but he does not hear them. The peasant women press against him speaking urgently of repeated floods, failed crops, hunger, death, of a sister who sits waiting with a crowd of women for her sister to die so they can parcel out her body for food, of that sister screaming in anger and fear and hunger that the other women have taken everything of her sister, leaving her only the head, but he hears only rapid, breathless mumblings because he thinks he does not understand their dialect, though he has glimmerings of their intentions, as if he were watching them through leaves from high above. The large sheet of paper is laid out on the red, polished countertop, and gently pulling his brush across the inkstone, twisting it slightly to charge his brush with blackness, he begins copying from memory Wang Xizhi's *Huang Ting* classic. He follows the seven character lines exactly, but his strokes are like black worms writhing on the page. Instead of the *Huang Ting* classic, he writes his father's autobiography, and closing the book unconcernedly, he washes out his brush in the pond below the stone bridge, letting the ink drip from the brush tip, meandering, black threads forming in the slow, moving water. Drip, drip, drop. Pure thought, unbidden, is like that, dreamlike and without anxiety, black strands of ink spreading slowly to catch up with the circling water, but tonight the dream does not pass on, it clings to him like a cap of silence. Wearing his black cap of silence, he hears the manslaughter case against Wei Siyong, who kidnaps his indentured servant Wei a-Kang's widowed daughter-in-law, also named Wei, from Wei a-Tu, to whom Wei a-Kang has sold her as a concubine, even though Wei Siyong had previously sold her to the wealthy business man Wei a-Guei, whose adherents now claim his due, but both transactions are unlawful because Wei a-Kang had indentured only himself and not his family, and his son and his son's wife Wei never lived with Wei a-Kang or submitted to Wei Siyong's service. In the rioting that follows, a man is killed. Who is at fault? What is at fault? The facts of the case spin like delicate jade gears in a *xüan ji* astronomical clock. Sitting in the night wearing his robe of darkness, he does not know who is at fault. What god would invent this kind of life for us? Or is it something we humans have invented for ourselves in order to be true to our singularly ignorant nature? He is not anxious. He feels no pain, no throbbing in his gigantic feet and melon hands, no alien sensation at all. Han Feizi invents a cylindrical casing armed with needles all around pointing inward, and to punish the inventor for his cruel imagination and to test the torture chamber, the emperor orders him placed in one of his own instruments. Han Feizi asks his keepers for brush and paper and writes a poem to the emperor. *Such is the path we follow, / between evening and the next day, / that we seem playthings of a dream. / Stop shivering, have patience; / thousand-armed fate strikes one family after another.* That night the emperor lays the poem aside. He sits in silent darkness at three in the morning, entombed in his own body.

So be it.

I.

APPENDIX

THE WANLI EMPEROR'S FIRST LETTER TO CERVANTES was written sometime between 1605 and 1612, and the extant fragments that I have discovered appear to be parts of a copy sent, either by special imperial messengers or by merchant caravans, along the ancient silk trail (which the emperor said was the path Christ followed into China): across the deserts and mountains of western Tian Shan and Chinese Turkistan to Samarkand, through Transoxiana and into Persia, straying across that vast area of unadministered central Asia that, for thousands of years, had been the passageway for mass conquests and migrations and home to hundreds of nomadic Mongolian, Tungusic, and Turkic tribes. This area was bound on the east by the growing power of the Khalkha Mongols in Outer Mongolia, by the Ordos and the Tümeds in Inner Mongolia, and by the China of Wanli. To the west and the north, the rapid growth of Muscovite territories beyond the Ural Mountains into Siberia under Ivan Groznyi—his conquest of the Kazans to their east and the Alans to their south—established an agricultural barrier to nomadism in the Russian steppes. South of this area, between the Caspian Sea and the mountains of Pamir, nomadic tribes were buffered from Safavid Persia by the khanates of Timur's descendants, in whose large trade cities, Samarkand, Bukhara, and Merv, sheep-skin-capped Sunnite Turksmen from between the Caspian and Aral seas brought their Shiite Persian captives to sell. Also to the south, between the Black and Caspian seas, Georgians, Caucasians, Azerbaijani, and Armenians were squeezed by the eastern reaches of the Ottoman Empire into the narrow valleys that sit between the 17,000-foot peaks of the Caucasian Range. An area of land the size of the United States, but without any large cities (Sarai, which once existed on the lower Volga, the most populous city of the Golden Horde, with a population of over half a million, having been destroyed by Timur in the fifteen century), it was, nonetheless, rich in the commotion and motion of human extravagances. This was the arena of Genghis Khan's activities, and here, on the borders of India and Persia, Genghis Khan wrote the Taoist alchemist monk Qiu Zhangchun of the golden lotus sect, begging him to come to Transoxiana to advise him on good governance, citing both the story of Wen Wang of the Zhou dynasty who, returning from the Wei River, met an old man fishing on the river whose conversation proved to be so wise that the future emperor took him home in his cart, as well as the story of Liu Bei, founder of the Shu Han dynasty, who sought the advice of Zhuge Liang, whom he found living in a reed hut, and so Qiu made the trip from Shandong and met with Genghis in Samarkand. The master was seventy years old then, but when he sat, his position was immovable, like that of a dead body, and when he stood upright, he resembled a tree; his movements were like thunder, and he walked like the wind. Other famous, infamous, and unknown travelers crisscrossed the immense wilderness on its many and long roads, the trade paths between the citified cultures at its peripheries, for gain, for adventure, for expansion of religion or power or for escape: German, Russian, Arabian, Persian, Italian, Chinese, Indian, and Tibetan merchants and craftsmen; messengers of the mighty; the friar John of Pian del Carpine and his companion Benedictus de Polon; William of Rubruck from Belgium, emissary of the King of France; the friar John of Montecorvino; Rabban Sauma and his companion Marcos; the Polos; outcasts either lowly like the heretical physician from Lombardy, whom John of Montecorvino met in Mongolia, or wielding great power, like Ala al-Din, the Grand Master of the hashish-smoking Ismaels or Assassins, whom Marco Polo called "Old Man of the Mountain"; the Roman Christian king George of the Onguts, who was deposed by his Nestorian Christian subjects in the fourteenth century; the isolated Khazars near the Black Sea, who gratuitously converted to Judaism in the eighth century; Tripitaka and his protectors Monkey, Sand, and Pig; the Byzantine ambassador Zemarcos; the Chinese pilgrims Xüan Zang, Yi Jing, and Wu Kung; and Caterina Viglioni, whose Latin tombstone testifies to her presence in Yangzhou in the thirteenth century. Buddhism, Judaism, Christianity, Islam, and all their sects, most extreme, overtook one another. Ethnic groups intermixed. Languages became confused.

During the Wanli period, the various tribes of the Oryat or Ölet Mongols of Inner Mongolia began massive migrations across this culturally and geographically open area. The Torguts left Chinese Turkistan in 1616, the year of Cervantes's death, to settle in the Volga river basin, where they were known as the Kalmuks, there to serve the Russian Tsar in his conquest of the Turkish tribes of the Caucasus. The Khoshot conquered Tibet and held all the high plateau areas from Burma to Ladakh. Under Galdan, the Dzungars established a huge state at the center of this nomadic whirl. In one way or another, the Oryats controlled the whole, vast region by the mid-eighteenth century, making them, at the time of the Boston Tea Party, perhaps the largest empire in the world, though as a nomadic culture, their rule was sporadic and without administration. The Russians and the Manchu dynasty of China sent repeated military expeditions against the Oryats throughout the eighteenth century, eventually subduing them. In 1772, partly because of Catherine the Great's attempt to turn the Kalmuks from nomadic herdsmen into plow-driving peasants, partly in order to escape the violence caused by Pugachov's Cossack rebellions and Russia's subsequent repressions, and partly because of continuing conflicts with neighboring Turkish tribes as well as with the Cossacks, who were part Turkish and part escaped serfs from throughout the Russian empire, 40,000 families of Kalmuks migrated east from south Russia back to China, only about half of whom survived the four-thousand mile trek and received lands in the Yili Valley from the Manchu Emperor Qian Long.

It was into this large kettle of human history that the Wanli Emperor's first letter to Cervantes disappeared, re-emerging in 1828 as flotsam on the western shore of the Caspian Sea. That year, the Azerbaijani poet Mirza Djan bought a packet of papers containing the fragments of the emperor's letter in the market of Baku as a piece of literary curiosity, these fragments being written in Arabic script, which he could not read, and the following year, he gave the papers, along with a letter explaining how he came upon them, as a going-away gift to the most famous writer he was likely to meet, the poet, playwright, and diplomat Aleksander

Sergeyevich Griboyedov, whose interest in oriental subjects was well known in Tiflis and who introduced both Pushkin and Lermontov to the theme.

Griboyedov, whose play *The Bitterness of Being Intelligent; or Woe from Wit* was known throughout the Russian empire, had successfully negotiated the Turkmenchai Treaty between Tsar Nicolas and Shah Feth-Ali of Persia, thus ending the war in Caucasia. He was only thirty-three years old and had married that year in Tiflis. He spoke and read Persian, having, in his early twenties, served in Teheran as the secretary of the Russian chief of mission, Sergei Ivanovich Mazarovich, the bastard son of the Italian admiral Giovanni Mazzaro; he was learning Caucasian; and he was preparing an oriental drama called *Rhadamiste and Zenobia*. He was bored in Tiflis, bored with being treated as a famous writer, bored with being asked to play the piano at social gatherings of wealthy German merchants because his sister was a famous pianist, but he was equally unhappy being sent as Minister Plenipotentiary to Persia to settle a further treaty dispute concerning the return of Russian subjects in Persian harems to Russia. On this trip, which took Griboyedov, accompanied by a one-hundred-horse guard from the forces of his friend General Ermolov, subduer of barbarians, from Tiflis to Erivan to Tabriz, through the high mountains between the Black Sea and the Caspian Sea, and then across northern Persia to Teheran, he wrote in his notebooks, "Flies, dust, and heat: one becomes an animal on this God-forsaken trail, which I'm following for the twentieth time." He tried to read the packet of papers Mirza Djan had given him, but though he knew Arabic script, he could not understand the language. In Teheran, he was treated royally, but he dealt harshly with Abdul-Hasan, the foreign minister for the Shah, living up to his Persian nickname *sachtir*, stone heart, and to emphasize his insistence that Russian subjects be returned, he accepted into the legation after the New Year the Armenian Mirza Yakoub, who had lived in Persia for over twenty years and was a convert to Islam, and who had been the Shah's finance minister, but who now asked for asylum and passage back to Armenia in Russian territory. Mirza Yakoub, much to the anger of Abdul-Hasan, moved into the Russian legation with his entourage, bringing with him two Armenian women who had fled from Persian harems and who were also given asylum.

On the evening of January 29th, 1829, Griboyedov ordered first secretary Maltsov to send a note to Abdul-Hasan informing him of his final decision to leave Teheran immediately with his charges. The next morning, aroused by the anti-Russian speeches that were being given at the mosques of Teheran, dozens of mobs from all over the city gathered in front the legation. The translator Chakhnazarov met them at the door with a contingent of guards and, after a single round of musket fire, was over-run. Griboyedov and a small group of guards retreated to the second floor, where they held off the crowd until the attackers broke through the roof and stoned the Russians to death. The only Russian to escape was the first secretary, Maltsov, who had not been in the legation at the time of the attack. On hearing of the massacre, he cleverly went to the Shah's palace, though he understood that the Shah had probably incited the mob, and asked for asylum, which was given him. Maltsov took charge of the situation almost immediately. He negotiated the Shah's apologies to the Tsar, wrote a report to St. Petersburg in which he stated that he was only able to recognize Griboyedov's body by the deformed little finger of his left hand, which had been shattered in a duel with Yakobovich, moved the legation to Tabriz, and sent Griboyedov's leather trunk and his body to Tiflis.

In one of the most famous passages in Russian literature, Pushkin relates that on June 11, 1829, he was walking near the fortress of Guerguery on Mount David:

> *I was crossing the river when I saw a pair of oxen pulling a crude, wooden cart up the steep hillside, attended by a group of Georgians.*

> *"Where are you coming from?" I asked them.*
> *"Teheran."*
> *"What have you got there?"*

"Griboyedov."

Griboyedov's widow lost their child at birth that year. She never remarried, devoted her life to organizing and publishing his papers, and when she died, she gave the collection to the Archives of Moscow, where Griboyedov had been born, and where it now forms part of the collection at the Russian State Library. Included therein is Mirza Djan's letter and the packet of Arabic writings, which Griboyedov scholars have ignored because it has nothing to do with the great writer and because it could not be read, being archaic Mongolian with mixtures of Chinese, Turkish, and Russian, though written phonetically in Arabic letters.

Obviously not the work of the *tung-wei* scribe, these fragments seem to indicate that the original letter was caught up in the great Torgut migration and taken into the Caucasus by some Kalmuk serving in the Russion expeditionary forces; that it was translated into Mongolian, probably fairly early, when some of the Torguts still understood Chinese, and that, further, the translation had been copied, perhaps more than once, by someone who did not understand the language, since the script shows enough deformations to suggest it was only graphically copied. Most probably the fragments were finally preserved by someone who was illiterate but who kept them for their presumed talismanic value, the paper showing signs of having been folded into a small container or sack. Such would be the simplest of the infinite histories one could construct for the letter.

In any case, when texts of one language are transliterated into the script of another, the translation difficulties are enormous. Not only does one script not phonetically match the sounds of another language, but these distortions are magnified by the obvious involvement of foreign speakers of both languages, with all their mishearings and mispronunciations and mistakes. One work that, by the very nature of its undertaking, is filled with such problems is Rashid Al-Din's *Jami al Tawarikh*, which was intended to be the first universal history (though obviously without mention of the Americas). In it, for example, we are told in Persian of the invasion of Egypt during the Sultanate of Malik Múazzam Turan-Shah by Afridis and of Afridis's subsequent capture. It seems that "Afridis" was Rashid Al-Din's corruption: Rashid being a Jewish convert and thus writing in Persian, in a foreign language, and addressing the Mongolian Khan of Persia, Oljeitu, for whom Persian was also a foreign tongue, and citing an Arabic source, which was in a language neither knew. In the Arabic chronicles of Egypt, the person Rashid Al-Din calls Afridis is called "El Raid Ifrans," which someone familiar with European history can recognize as a phonetic rendering of the French "le roi de France," for, as Joinville recounts, in 1248, Louis IX, otherwise known as Saint Louis, was captured in Egypt by the Saracen sultan. Rashid himself was fully aware of and constantly discussed this problem of deriving words and names through a process of misunderstanding or mispronunciations—the Mongolians, for example, use the Turkish *ot* and *tegin*, meaning "lord of the hearth," to refer to the youngest son, who is traditionally charged with taking care of the family yurt, but, because they are unable to make the double *t* sound, they end up saying *otchegin* instead, or *otchi* for short, which, ironically, is a possible source for the Russian word for father—so that Rashid's universal history is a sapid description of the Babel of tongues out of which we humans make our lives meaningful.

Even without this difficulty of dealing with foreign sounds, alphabets don't represent speech sounds very well, and in time, pronunciations change and sometimes letters do too, making for strange combobulations. Take, for example, the *x* in Quixote's name: Cervantes meant that letter to represent something of a sh-sound, hazily preserved in the French version, *Don Quichotte*. But if you go to Spanish bookstores, you will find that his name is *Don Quijote*, because the Royal Spanish Academy, attempting to purify the language in the eighteenth century, changed the Greek *x* to a Latinate *j*, reserving *x* for the *ks*-sound in mostly foreign words. Unfortunately, the letter *j* evolved into a fricative *h*-sound, made more towards the back of the tongue, changing the pronunciation of Don Quixote's name in Spanish. Yet in English we keep the *x* and have no idea how to say it, the late, eminent critic Alfred Kazin insisting that we say *kwiksot* since we say *Meksico*, for no reason at all, while the Castilian speaking Mexican says *Mehico*, and the original Mexican said *Meshico*.

Thus the translations of Mirza Djan's discovery are problematic, to say the least. Further, the evidence that these fragments formed parts of the Wanli Emperor's letter is not strong, though the salutation "Dear Mi Hai" as well as the signature "I" survived and are thus suggestive. Words implying a twentieth-century setting in Armenia, or is it Armorica or America, are bizarre, though textual obfuscation and mistranslations might explain them. Given this uncertainty, I have relegated these fragments to the appendix and present them here without further commentary.

THE EMPEROR'S FIRST LETTER TO CERVANTES

Dear Mi Hai,

I have read . . . .

. . . .

. . . she held onto Daisy's hand while they edged crab-
wise down the steep sidewalk behind Suzy, all three
laughing hysterically while trying to hop and counter-
balance their sliding high heels, jerking this way and
that, arms waving, their bared legs stretching tight the
sheaths of their slit dresses, light summer silk dresses,
hers a pale blue one with small, hardly perceptible
square embossing, tailored with the low and soft collar
she always insisted upon. . . . but the Peaceable North
where they had been schoolmates and college-mates
had no such steep hills. She held Suzy's, not Daisy's
hand, swinging it high as they crossed to the wharf side
of the street. . . . or so it seemed, though she knew she
had never been there with Suzy and Daisy. . . . glowed
in the shadowed streets from the sunset reflecting off
the tall, rising buildings that faced the harbour, as if the
waterfront were lit with stage lights. Now they were
standing still, listening to the sailor speak. She held
Suzy's hand tightly. Now we were running, watched
by the three sailors, she told Eddie, whom she called

Charlie, confusing him with his brother and uncertain which had married Suzy and which Daisy, Suzy and Eddie, Daisy and Charlie, or Suzy and Charlie, Daisy and Eddie, though it didn't matter, because Suzy was her best friend, not Daisy, who was just Suzy's sister, and Charlie and Eddie came later. . . .

. . . .

. . . emotions last longer than thoughts. Long after she had forgotten the names of the enzymes that presided over the hundreds of reactions that transformed the masticated lump of wet rice in her mouth into the cellular energy that kept her alive, she still conjured up with each mouthful satisfying admiration for the clarity and neatness of the chemistry of her digestion, and though what she'd claimed about the leak under her sink had become as uncertain as my sarcastic rejoinder that it was only condensation, her indignation and humiliation made her breath catch in a sob every time she looked at me across the small, oval dining table. After a lifetime of thinking about how to overcome the terrible *techne* of existing day after day, the feeling of wisdom had outlasted its application. Not having seen a hammer until she was well past thirty-five, not having thought of its function, and having had to learn the word for the first time when she stood dazzled by the array of arcane objects displayed in the hardware store, she was understandably proud when she carried home her new hammer—name, meaning, function, and object conjoined as a single idea—and drove her first nail home, satisfied with her acquisition. It was part of this new land, the new culture, the new language she had come to and for which she seemed to have prepared all her life, seemed because her life had been a series of difficulties triumphed over by her independence and intelligence, but now that her life had pulled in its edges, shying away even from her own body, away from that reality I kept insisting she pay attention to, that preparation had become futile as her past formed her only immediacy, her land both old and new.

The glories and frustrations of her life rolled through her daily sentiments without surfacing in memory as images, stories, or meaning, at times making her cry out in anger as if she were again struggling with the purse-snatcher in downtown Singapore while a traffic policeman in the intersection calmly ignored her screams, but having forgotten the incident itself, she wondered at her outburst. At other times, she grinned broadly at some secret but unknown pleasure.

Forgetting made her life more unified, the various moments now a single experience. Once, years ago, she'd been surprised by a memory of her father's laughing account of himself as a young snob in Beijing intellectual circles when he first came back from overseas wearing a jaunty fedora and smoking American cigarettes. She remembered him smiling and chuckling with self-assurance at his youthful follies and imagined the great distance between that middle-aged, prosperous bureaucrat in his grey silk scholar's robe and the insolent, cravated boy of his story, but at that time she herself had passed middle age, and, remembering her father telling the story, she was surprised at her own memories of Daisy and Suzy, her best friends in college, Daisy, who dared her to be the first girl to major in Physics, which she had done, partly because the Physics professor was a young, blonde American, or was he British, surprised that her memories of her college days were not at all distant from her as she had imagined her father being distant from his past, but instead seemed all of one piece with her present. She did not know if she had a mistaken impression of her father—or, indeed, of other people in general—or whether people were themselves as continuous as she felt herself to be, as if she never got old, as if time were simply a facet of that crystalline, exterior world, or if she simply had a stronger self-conceit. Other people complained about growing older, but she never felt it to be a problem except physically, her eyesight blurring, the cataracts having to be removed, leaving her those artificial eyes she had to feel for every morning, feeling around the bedside table, her slightly bent, knobby, arthritic fingers outstretched, touching everything lightly so as not to knock anything over, her hearing deteriorating until she could no longer make out the sharp, brittle sounds of her granddaughter's voice on the phone, every holiday a tiresome series of *what did you say, what, say that again but not so loud, how are your ducks, I said,* but such bodily handicaps became, through repetition, more and more forgotten, and then she felt even more alien from those American women who always whined to her about the passing years. Then she forgot that surprising discovery about herself, and she forgot the question it had brought to her mind, but she retained her feeling of difference, and she felt even stronger the lack of any temporality in herself.

Dinner over, she carefully stacked the bowls, emptied to the last grain of rice, set the bowls without a sound on the stacked plates, and, saying to me *No, no, no, you go watch television, you cook, I'll do the dishes,* to me who was beating the detergent into a sinkful of water with chopsticks, she lowered her stack of dishes into the warm water with both hands. It was wasteful, so much water to wash a few bowls and plates. Her way of using only a small bowlful of soapy water with a thin stream of water from the faucet for rinsing was much better, but he stubbornly refused to do anything her way.

She had outgrown her own language, had become disarticulated, not like her children, whose disarticulation was a matter of never having had a native language, of having been forced always to speak a foreign tongue as if it were their own, but rather disarticulated by never having learned her new language well enough to maintain it into the reveries of old age. Yet the only language she did speak was an artificial and dead one, now at least fifty years out of date, spoken by no one else in the world, understood only by a few, and those few on the other side of the world, so that when she wrote her younger sister, whom she could not remember ever seeing, she laboriously looked up every character in a new dictionary, sometimes breaking out in laughter to rediscover an old phrase *(e zi, hai, how could I have forgotten the word, perhaps I'd never seen any moths when I was in China),* but many times puzzled by the simplifications of the writing, *hai, they've made everything look the same.* Sometimes there were things she wanted to tell him but could only conjure them up as desires or images so long held in her body that her muscles seemed more able to act them out than her mouth could speak them. Sometimes, however, her disarticulation seemed more important, hindering her thinking process, entangling her thoughts in a mesh of broken phrases in several languages and abruptly halting them in deep lacunae. Then she felt nauseous, a ball of emptiness in her stomach, and helpless.

. . . .

. . . saw the man looking at her across the large table,

facing her, his forearms resting in front of him, his hands outstretched, flat on the empty tabletop, and saw him slowly wipe his arms outward across the table and bring them together again, crossing the jointure of the drop-leaf, a delicate jointure, overlapped, not butted but rounded, fitted and overlapped like a linearly drawn-out version of a human knee or elbow whose polished inner surfaces might be imagined as a kind of easy and continuous motion, but having felt so slowly the contours of this rich, amber-stained maple, she was unable to look again at the man in front of her. She could no longer distinguish his face. Only his arms lay languidly stretched out towards her, as if he had been decapitated, and, straining to look up at where his head ought to have been, she realized that she did not remember why she had conjured up this image, only that there had been a reason, perhaps as an argument against her son, but what argument, what point, perhaps as a manifestation of a seer who could explain something to her, but what, perhaps a memory of some significant event, but all of it had dissipated, she could only remember the joint on the drop-leaf that now, having lost its marvelous clarity, seemed not unlike the kitchen table where she ate her meals day after day. Her thoughts died within her in this way, became static, lifeless, and piecemeal, her inner world distracted into dissipation, the familiar patterns of associative daydreaming broken up into fitful, flat images. . . .

....

... flagellated each other, but their shares were not equal, since she merely repeated those taunts about my stupidity, calling me dumb or ignorant, which she had at one time in my life said jokingly, teasing my childish pride, but which now, in repetition, cut me deeply, while for my part, I, who was sane, struggled to magnify my violations of her, calling her old, insane, selfish, *no wonder your own children hate you,* such gross exaggerations that I could never take any of it back and so expended myself, morally revealing myself in my exhaustion, so that afterward I cringed at my audacity, while she merely forgot it all or fabricated the event, wove it into the fabric of the cultural clichés she had imbibed during twenty years of watching television, a foreigner gladly absorbing the native culture, thus attributing my anxiety and alcoholism to worry over my teenage daughter's wild flings with her high-school teachers.

....

... saw on the studio porch the sturdy, thick-walled pot that my mother had made, covered with red clay drippings and heavy, and it recalled to me my mother prevaricating between her finicky and not innate pleasure in formal beauty and quiet and her utilitarian desire, transcendent of ego, to make use of everything, beautiful or not, fitting or not, a conflict and a balance, perhaps, that made her sigh characteristically when she finally rejected this pot, casting it out of the studio to be used for her clay slip, and, having recalled this enlivened image of my mother, I wondered whether I ought not clean up the pot and bring it inside the house so as to have a memento of her, but as soon as I considered such a preservation, in violation of her will, the mystery of her life overwhelmed me, as did the mystery of her death, and I felt how weak and faulty my memory was in trying to contain that mystery. It seemed to me then that Shakespeare had been so juvenile and naive when he seriously proposed that he could defeat death by being remembered. He must not have forgotten as much as I. . . .

. . . .

Down the hallway, the lines converging in the shadowless but colorless, dim-like-an-ancient-memory hospital corridor, a man sat diagonally blocking the way in a wooden school chair, a clip-board on the chair's writing arm, and when he looked up, she recognized him, glad that this almost senseless wandering down the corridors of the ophthalmologist's office was, after all, directed and intended, because she suddenly remembered that when she had been left alone for a moment by both the nurse and the doctor, she had escaped the examining chair, her vision blurred by the dilating Tropicamide, remembered that she had intended to search for the hospital laboratory where the ophthalmologist was to send the exudate from her eye for analysis, and here he was, the lab technician, sitting cross-legged in this old-fashioned school chair at a crossing in the corridors of some hospital, smiling at her familiarly and greeting her, "Hello, hello, it's been so many years since I saw you last," and reassuring her, "Nothing wrong at all, no infection, negative, nothing, the doctor was fooling you." *They cannot fool me. I know the people in the lab. I went there, though nobody knows, the time you took me to the eye doctor's. You had to leave to get dog food, so you don't know how I stole out of the examining room, turning to the left and then the other way.* The corridor was very wide, dark stripes along the walls, the wallpaper bumpy and plastic to her touch, walking down a long, wide hallway that was all lit up, though she could not tell where the light came from, and *then I turned, let's see, this way and went down another corridor, very far, until I reached the lab* that she knew very well and has for many years, somewhat over a mile from the ophthalmologist's office. At the end of the corridor, double-glass doors led to a small room with two blacktopped tables along two facing walls. *The lab technician in a white coat recognized me, he knows me well, and he told me not to worry, nothing wrong with me, the tests are all negative, but just to make sure, they made me take my clothes off for an examination. While I was behind the curtain, I heard them talking about your book. He lent you a book.*

. . . .

He cleans out the mold from the drawer and is saddened. The spotted, mildewed binder papers, cardboard cut from tea boxes, old bills scribed with leaf and flower patterns or scribbled on the backs with calculations of concentrations for various mixtures of minerals used to achieve different color glazes, foxed and pungent pamphlets on ceramic ovens, bent, fired cones used to test oven temperatures, a torn corner of a calendar where she had written his name to remind herself that these were all plans for the tiles she was making for him to cover the fireplace in his new house, and, at the bottom of the drawer, the source of the mold, dozens of broken pieces of thallophytes and weeds she had collected to use as models for her designs. Laid out in the sun on the garden ledge, they seemed to him to dispel their gracious intentionality as they slowly gave up their spores to the summer breeze. She had never finished the project, lacking only three tiles for the set when she finally forgot what she was doing after having spent several years on it. In the other drawer, he found a black leather-covered notebook that had once belonged to his father but which he had used as a diary when, at the age of twelve, he had traveled with the Scouts to a national jamboree, the smeared, old-fashioned ballpoint ink lines jutting about the page in ways so familiar that the childish scrawl looked more his than his present handwriting, as if some spectroscopy had revealed the skeletal frame upon which hung the rounded flesh of his hand, and even the boyish patter of the words themselves—*after that we played around, I played a game of Chess with our patrol leader, he beat me, I started out good but I got careless and lost my queen*—seemed the ghostly sketch of an image that had been thoroughly over-painted and finished but still the essential *eidos* of his identity, the outline of his life's story. And under the mildewed, grey notebook was a large, black paper box, an Indian head on its label, which he immediately recognized as the box in which had come his baseball mitt, the one whose fingers he tied together with rawhide to make the mitt hold a more natural pocket, the one he pounded hour after hour with his hardball and his clenched fist to stretch the pocket deeper, the one he rubbed Vaseline and neatsfoot oil into daily, the one he tied the ball into every night to shape it, the one he heated in the oven to make the leather absorb more oil, but inside the box was no mitt, he knew, only some small pieces of wood, buttons, hairpins, and another box he immediately recognized as the original container for one of the two telegraph keys he and his mother had bought together at the Army surplus store in Sacramento and which they had rigged with batteries and door buzzers so he could learn the Morse code for his merit badge, sending messages back and forth in the mornings from their bedrooms. The box was empty. He handled these things she had saved from his childhood, wondering at the mystery this woman had been and still was to him and astonished at the feelings of loss and emptiness these objects called him to.

So be it.

I.

MAX YEH, author of the novel *The Beginning of the East*, was born in China, educated in the United States and has lived in Europe and Mexico. He has taught at the University of California, Irvine, Hobart and William Smith Colleges, and New Mexico State University. He lives in the New Mexico mountains with his wife and daughter, where he works on a wide range of subjects including literary theory, linguistics, art history, and science.